KOZLOV CHRONICLES

STITCHED

ELENA SOBOL

Copyright © 2022 by Elena Sobol. All rights reserved. No portion of this book may be reproduced in any form without permission from the publisher, except as permitted by U.S. copyright law. No part of this book may be used or reproduced in any manner whatsoever without written permission except in the case of brief quotations embodied in critical articles or reviews. This book is a work of fiction. Names, characters, places, events and incidents are either the product of the author's imagination or are used fictitiously. Any resemblance to actual persons, living or dead, events, or locales, are entirely coincidental.

Author website: www.elenasobol.net

Front Cover: coversbychristian.com

Editing: copybykath.com

If you want to be notified of Elena Sobol's new books, get free stories and occasional other goodies, please sign up for her mailing list by going to: www.elenasobol.net Your email address will never be shared and you can unsubscribe at any time.

1

WHEN YOU GIVE A demigod a beer, he will drink for a day. When you teach a demigod to brew, he will get humans drunk for the duration of his long, *long,* life.

Not that I was much older than these college kids who drank like it *wasn't* Wednesday. Relieving my tray, I slid plastic pitchers across the table. A beat-poet type took a sip of his Hefeweizen. His eyes widened behind thick glasses.

"Duude," he said, throwing a look at his orange-haired date. "This is the best hef I've ever had."

I grinned. "House recipe," I lied. The truth was that the bar shipped that swill here from Idaho. It tasted amazing because I had enchanted the mugs myself. Fishing for tips, I flashed a smile at Orange Hair.

"You should try the mead."

Hi, I'm your local Utah demigod of the harvest, and I have the best job in the world.

"Dmitry!" my manager's voice pierced my ears. "Order up!

I threw the towel over my shoulder and hurried over to collect the order before she got pissy.

The Salty Dog Brewery was hopping for a weekday and I caught an irritated glance from my manager, Tricia. She loved giving me a hard time. Scowling, she loaded my tray with more mugs and a martini glass full to the brim with something artificially pink. I touched each mug. The second my fingers touched the glass, I felt the bubbles and flavors inside. I repaired them all—balance, depth, and alcohol content. I left the pink abomination alone. Not even a god could save that.

My fellow server, Kiki, passed me, her toned arms carrying a tray full of nachos and cocktails with enviable grace. If I said that her etched dancer's shoulders, beautifully displayed by her revealing tank, didn't make my throat wobble, that would be a big ole Texas lie. She smiled with a row of straight, white teeth.

"The Bloody Mary bar could use the Dmitry touch," she said. Her French accent made "touch" sound like "tush." My toes tingled. Damn, that accent would make anyone drop their penny. God bless Senegal.

I saluted her. "Ma'am, yes, ma'am."

Her dark eyes dropped to my jeans. "Do you have to carry those around?"

I glanced down. A pair of ancient knitting needles stuck out of my back pocket. My fingers circled around them protectively.

I winked at Kiki. "How else would I make you look at my butt?"

She laughed and left me to refill the tomato mix and vodka. When no one was looking, I transferred the needles from my back pocket to under my shirt. Losing them could cost me my life. And I wasn't about to get eaten by a back-alley werewolf when I'd worked so hard to stop my own family from killing me.

The lid on the gallon of lime concentrate was ajar. I sniffed at it and cringed at the vinegary stench. Some idiot had left it open and it had turned rancid. I was that idiot. Hefting the gallon, I headed for the back door.

The sun was low in the sky, and the June air smelled like linden blossoms. I breathed deeply. The Salty Dog had been my home ever since I turned twenty-one, five years ago. I never wanted another human job. Next week, after years of saving, I would sign documents for a small warehouse of my own. I would start a legitimate brewery. As long as the human law didn't get a clue that my "small" basement brewing operation was much bigger than what I claimed on my taxes. Or, my older cousin, Golo, didn't finally find me and marinate me in the marshes of Vyraj, the Slavic pantheon. So far, I'd dodged them both for a decade. #Winning!

The drain grate reflected the lights of the parking lot. Careful not to breathe in, I poured out the bottle. I watched the goo disappear, grateful to be alive to brew another day. I'd lived in Utah for twelve years. Outside of the occasional fairy raid on my garden, or a drunk vodyanoi crashing my roommate's party, I was largely undisturbed by the creatures of Vyraj. Most of the supernaturals that lived in Salt Lake City had their own problems and their own families to dodge. They didn't care who I really was, or who was looking for me. The only other supernatural presence was the Spiral, a sort of extra-scary universal police that had an office downtown Salt Lake City. As the guardians of the human plane—or Yav, or Midgard, or Gaia, depending on what you believed—they had never taken an interest in me. There was a reason my famous grandmother sent me here when I was a kid. Who the hell would look for a brewing demigod among Mormons?

As I reached for the door handle, I heard the click-clacks of little nails against the asphalt. I turned around in time to see a blue shape shooting across the parking lot like a bullet. Behind it, a rippling tear in the universe bent the light of the setting sun. Its edges sparked with electricity. I recognized an inter-pantheon portal. The blue shape blurred closer, and I recognized a familiar noodely body.

The ferret looked frantic. Its fur was ruffled like it'd been through a spin cycle. Before I could do more than squeal like a girl, it scampered up my leg. Its—her—tail curled around my throat. She trembled.

"Alysa." I ran a comforting hand over her soft fur. "What are you doing here?"

A growl and a sucking noise snapped my attention back to the portal. Something that looked like lumps of muscles and joints fell out of the edges. Short-snouted, ape-like faces scowled at me with rows of yellow teeth. The empty bottle I still held fell to the ground and shattered. Backing into the door, I had the presence of mind to grope for the handle and pull.

"I gotta take a ten!" I yelled into the opening.

I slammed the door shut and slid the outer bolt in place.

"Hang on to me," I said to the ferret. Chattering, she dug her nails into my shirt. My hands fumbled for my needles. I drew them out, feeling the magic pulse in the ancient copper. An ear-splitting scream came from one of the creatures when it spotted the ferret around my shoulders. Instantly, I knew what I was dealing with.

Drekavacs, the screamers, were supposedly born of babies who died before baptism. Or so the misguided monotheists of

Yugoslavia believed. In reality, they were nasty little goblins who were eating corpses way before Christianity stomped through the Old World with its iron boots.

The monsters came pouring out of the portal like a gang of angry monkeys. I counted five, all no taller than my hip. The real danger came from their muscles and claws that were made for tearing flesh. Their eerie baby demon mugs cackled when they saw a kid in an apron holding up two knitting needles. I might as well have rung the dinner bell.

"Give usss the shifterrr," they cooed in Old Slav as they circled. "She will diiie. You will liiive."

"Orrr," another joined in, his teeth dripping with saliva. "You bottth diiie."

My palms burned with energy as the knitting needles swelled in my hands. Two daggers glistened where the needles used to be. I flicked my wrists, and the blades caught the setting sun. Sila and Veter, Power and Wind, were comforting weights in my hands.

"Orrr," I mocked. "You realize that you crashed the wrong parking lot."

I dropped into a crouch as the first monster came at me. Its teeth snapped over my head. Thrusting up Sila, I opened its belly. The dagger cut through the creature like wire through lard. Its black blood sprayed me and stained my Salty Dog t-shirt. Damn it, I'd just washed it!

The drekavac behind him screamed a blood-curdling version of a baby's cry and set out to avenge his friend. Gaining speed, he pushed off with powerful legs and shot at me with the menace of a cannon ball. With Alysa riding the roller coaster of my shoulders, I rolled out of the way. The creature thudded against the back door. It fell, leaving a boulder-sized dent. Their pin-prick eyes red with anger, the three remaining drekavacs stared. The easy prey they had expected was turning out to have teeth of its own.

I wiped my bloody dagger on my apron and grinned. "Whoops." The blue ferret disappeared under the collar of my shirt.

The three remaining drekavacs did exactly what I expected them to—they split up to flank me. While one headed me straight on, the others shot at me from the sides. When they landed, claws out, I was no longer there.

Leaping over the head of my shorter assailant, I planted my feet behind him. I twisted my torso, daggers parallel, and buried them at the base of his neck and spine. The creature howled. I caught another drekavac on the ribs as he rushed me and left a gaping wound along his side. His teeth drew blood on my forearm. Retaliating, I wrenched Sila out of his friend and stabbed him between the eyes. The drekavac dropped.

The third creature paced back and forth while his friends died. His grotesque features turned from blood-lust to uncertainty. When I wrenched Sila out of the one that had tried to get me from the side, he backed up to the portal, turned and ran. True to its name, Veter, the wind dagger, whirled after him. It pierced his heart like an apple. I felt the pull through the fabric of realities as the daggers connected. Following the golden thread between them, I materialized on the other side and caught Veter's handle. I was just in time to see the drekavac collapse in a pool of its own blood. This was when I saw I'd miscalculated. There were not five drekavacs; there were six.

The last one had hung back in the shadows and watched his friends die. Now, he was sprinting toward the portal. I cocked Veter, then shrugged and lowered it. It was just the one, what was the harm? With a hateful look of its beady eyes, the creature bared its teeth and leapt through the edges.

A soft ball stirred in the sleeve of my shirt. The blue ferret slid out of it like a hairy python. She shook out her body and looked up at me in reprimand. Blurring, she swelled on the asphalt until her shape grew to the size of a girl. A pair of grumpy green eyes stared at me through the mess of bubblegum-blue hair.

"Sew it shut!"

I felt like I'd missed a sitcom episode. "Eh?"

"The portal, Dmitry!" she insisted. "Sew it shut with the needles."

I glanced down and saw that my daggers had slimmed down to the size of a pair of knitting needles. The golden thread of Fate hummed between them. Not sure what I was doing, I stumbled to the sizzling portal. Through it, I could smell pines and pond lilies. The sight of Vyraj's pink sky made me panic. I'd spent the last ten years trying to stay as far from my home as I could, and now there it was. A stone's throw away and crawling with creatures—and demigods—that wanted to kill me. A gust of wind pulled me forward until I realized that the portal itself was tugging at my hair and sucking at my shirt. It wanted me to step through. Screw that.

I caught the two sparkling edges of the portal with my needles. The golden thread drew the gash closed and the entrance between the two worlds disappeared with a pop.

"What," I panted, "the hell was that?"

"That was the third portal I found," Alysa said. "In Salt Lake. This week."

Goosebumps of apprehension crawled up my arms. My human home had been safe for years. This was the last thing I needed.

"So?" I asked, trying to swallow my jolt of panic.

"So," she mocked, "we're *both* screwed if we don't find the asshole who's opening the portals to Vyraj."

2

"BIG RACCOONS," I TOLD Tricia. My arms stretched out wide. "Mega huge."

My manager and I loitered in the velvet dusk. Only minutes before, Alysa and I had dragged the drekavacs off to the nearest dumpster. Tricia's phone flashed between the parking lot and the back door. She eyed me suspiciously and I tried looking as innocent as a Slavic face allowed. Her pinched expression told me she wasn't buying it. My bicep still bled, but luckily that could pass for an animal attack.

"Bob's gonna kill me," she said sourly. "Thanks."

"Huge raccoons!" I shook my hands for emphasis. "Can't fuck with nature, man."

She rubbed her freckled forehead. "You should've followed them to their nest. We need to call animal control, and you didn't even see where they went. They'll just keep coming back."

I shrugged. "Defending the homestead is priority number one."

She looked at me with distaste. "God, you're weird."

I'd take "weird" over "let's get some pitchforks and meet in the town square." Good thing drekavacs' blood was so dark it barely showed on the asphalt. Since they didn't belong in Yav, their corpses—and the evidence of supernatural—would turn to goo in the dumpster in a matter of hours. That's why most humans had no idea another world existed. Once dead, most of it was too fragile to take to authorities.

I plucked at my tattered shirt. "I gotta go home. Can't go back out on the floor looking like this."

To my surprise, my hard-ass manager nodded as she texted Bob, the owner. "Fine. But you're covering for Kiki next week."

Hardly believing my luck, I started across the parking lot to where Alysa was waiting for me.

"Hey!" Tricia called after me. "Don't forget to get a rabies shot, you dumb ass!"

Alysa sat on the sidewalk next to my alligator-green Mazda. Her face was burrowed into a bag of pistachios from my glove compartment. Her jeans were torn at the knees, and her blue BYU alumni t-shirt was black on the shoulder. She brushed her blue hair off her forehead. Her forehead was tall and her nose was a cute upturned button. I glanced around to make sure no one was watching us. A muscled young guy standing over a cute girl who looked like a kidnapping victim? I'd call the cops on me. I saw a middle-aged man in a bright-yellow shirt loading groceries into his car across the street. A pin glinted on his chest. It caught the light of the parking lot lamps and briefly blinded me. He pulled the hat over his eyes and continued to close the trunk.

"These are stale," Alysa complained into the half-empty bag.

"Right," I said. "That's why you ate most of them." I leaned against the driver door.

"Thanks for the rescue," she said. "They would've torn me apart."

I shrugged. "I doubt that. You're hard to catch. Do you need a ride home?"

Alysa lived in a small town south of Salt Lake City called Midway. She ran a coffee shop called Blue Ferret Cafe. The name was a little on the nose, but the coffee was excellent. And those lavender muffins? Yum.

She scoffed. "As if I need you to drive me anywhere. I'm a portal, remember?" She snapped her fingers. "Boom, and I'm home."

"Yep. Good. So talented." I said, trying not to sound too eager to get rid of her. I needed to go home and double my wards. No, triple them. My domovoi, the house spirit who I unimaginatively called Domo, had to be informed immediately. He was my home security and the reason I could sleep at night.

She licked her fingers. "I'm coming with you. We're going to figure out this portal situation."

I crossed my arms. "We? I've got a bootleg empire to protect. Besides, you're the living portal to Vyraj. If someone is opening pathways to Yav," I said, using the ancient Slavic name for the human world, "you'll find them. Their magic has to be incredibly strong." I squinted, imagining what it would take to tear through so many layers of reality. "God-like, actually."

"That's the problem." Alysa stood up and dusted off her jeans. She let the bag drop to the ground. Litter bug. "I can't sense anyone opening them when I'm in Vyraj. And here..." She searched for words. "They're elusive, like they're warded somehow. I can't sense them." She shook her head. "I don't know. Besides," she cocked her head at the darkening sky, her smile sly, "you wouldn't leave a girl to her own devices in the middle of the night, would you?"

She fluttered her eyelashes at me like a damsel in distress. I cocked an eyebrow, then pressed the unlock button on my car keys.

"Fine," I relented. "James would hate me if I didn't bring you to his party, anyway."

I drove home in a sulk, while Alysa rifled through my car's compartments for snacks. The two-story Craftsman house I shared with my roommate, James, was alive with lights and music. Beats pulsed between the square columns of the porch. People were smoking out front and I heard their chatter as we pulled up. I recognized James' band members as I killed the engine. They were a loud, social bunch that would immediately pull me into a drunken conversation.

"Come on," I said to Alysa. "We're sneaking in the back."

We climbed the stone path that led to the back gate. Rows of tomatoes, squash, cucumbers and melons greeted us. We ducked under an archway supporting a small explosion of concord grapes and I breathed in the green, fertile air of my garden's micro-climate. Domo's wards closed behind us. Now, supernatural beings couldn't sense our presence from the street. The stress of the evening eased out of my shoulders. I was home, and among growing things I had nurtured myself. I could figure this out. No one knew I was here. I just needed to fortify our house's defenses and go to ground for a couple of months. Just until this portal business blew over.

Alysa eyed the vines that choked the life out of every trellis and fence post in sight. "Don't you think your grapes are a little out of control?"

I grinned. "Wait till you see the tomatoes."

Through the sliding porch door, I could see into the kitchen. It was empty. James must've been playing his guitar in the living room. I usually left the back door unlocked. I mean, we lived in Utah. I jerked the handle and found it firmly shut. I crouched and searched under the mat for the spare key.

A face that looked like it was covered in two weeks of grime, and an improbable amount of hair, peered at me through the glass door. I fell back on my ass.

"You may not pass," the creature hissed, in a three-foot-tall impression of Gandalf. Except that he spoke in Old Slav. "With Koschei's cursed portal."

3

"THAT'S JUST RUDE, DOMO," Alysa said over my head. "I'm the reason you live with Dmitry in the first place."

The domovoi hissed up at her through the glass.

"Come on," I pleaded with the house spirit. "We've been through this. Alysa is not a threat to this house. It's been years since she's been Koschei's subject." I spoke in the Old Slav with him, even though my pronunciation was atrocious. "You're supposed to protect the house from intruders. Intruders, Domo. Just let us in."

"But, master, what would your grandmother say?" The domovoi gave me a puppy dog stare. His owlish eyes just made him look more terrifying. "Koschei the Deathless is her enemy."

Veles eternal, it was like living with your bigot grandpa. I resorted to a bribe. "I'll buy you more chanterelles. Pickled mushrooms." I wiggled my eyebrows.

Domo's face lit up. "And more mouse traps."

"You drive a hard bargain." I tapped on the glass. "Come on, it's chilly out."

With a face that told me I'd find a dead cockroach in my slipper tomorrow, he unlatched the glass door. I stepped through and into the warmth of the house.

"Thanks, Domo," I turned back to the spirit and saw that he was gone. It was no surprise. James' music and laughter was approaching a deafening degree. His disapproval delivered, the noise-hating domovoi had immediately bounced.

Alysa slid the door closed behind us. "Finally. I need a shower."

"It smells like a sweat lodge down here," she complained as we descended to the basement portion of the house. Casa de Dmitry.

I grinned. "Welcome to the most amazing basement in the world."

Humidity hung in the air and plants filled every surface. Vines cascaded down tables and the scent of dill intermingled with the coriander and mint. A hardy cluster of Venus fly traps—my favorite—opened their yawning little mouths. I took special pride in being able to grow them better than any greenhouse in the country. Of course, the smell that Alysa was complaining about came from the cement portion of the basement where the shelves were lined with fermenters. Of various sizes and shapes, they bubbled with happy yeast, turning sugar to alcohol. I breathed in deeply and smiled. Ah, the smell of my illegal brewing operation.

"Sorry about Domo," I said.

Alysa snorted. "I don't care. If I had a domovoi casting wards over my home, he could be as nasty as he wanted."

Domo had snuck into my backpack on my one and only trip to Vyraj since I was fourteen years old. It was also the time I met Alysa. He'd been living with me ever since.

I pulled a bottle of strawberry wine off the shelf. "How about a glass of the best rosé in the state?"

Alysa gave me a tired look. "Very humble." I wiggled my eyebrows, and she sighed. "Shower, first."

She waited while I found some clothes that would fit her. I folded up a teddy bear t-shirt an ex had left, and a pair of sweats that had shrunk in the wash. Alysa took them and a fresh towel and disappeared through the bathroom door.

I poured myself a glass and stripped off my bloodied shirt. Standing in front of a floor-length mirror, I used a first aid kit to clean the tear on my shoulder. The laceration didn't look infected, but I gritted my teeth and dabbed it with alcohol anyway. After bandaging the cut, I gave myself a quick once-over to check for bruises. I was no Rock, but I always made sure that my love for beer was compensated for by my time in the gym with my buddy, Min-Ho. With Alysa occupying the bathroom where I had my one and only comb, I ran my fingers through my hair. My dark blond undercut needed a trim. I did my best to smooth the longer hair on top and let it fall to my right ear. I found a shirt on my bed, sniffed it, and pulled it over my head.

On my table, the contract for a small warehouse sat unsigned. I had scraped and saved every penny over the last five years for a down payment. Now, the single floor green beauty with proper plumbing and plenty of space for vats was almost mine. My good mood returned with a vengeance. Once I assured Alysa that there was nothing I could do for her, I would get everything under control. No pesky Vyraj creatures were going to sneak in here to disclose my location to my cousins. I wouldn't have *this* house burned to the ground.

I was feeling refreshed and mellow with my glass of rosé when Alysa's face poked out from behind the bathroom door. Her azure hair dripped into a towel she pressed to her head. Droplets of water clung to her shoulders. Steam accompanied her sudden appearance, and I gulped more wine to keep my brain from imagining what was hiding behind the narrow plank of wood. We were friends, damn it. Friends don't ogle friends.

"Don't think that we're done talking," she announced. "This is serious, Dmitry. If we don't find the portal opener, our precious Utah will be in jeopardy."

I swirled the wine in my glass. With Alysa in my shower and the gentle nudge of wine telling me to relax and kick back, I was feeling pretty good. "Maybe it's not caused by anyone. Maybe it's like a... natural occurrence, you know?"

"Yeah, like Global Warming?" she said sourly. "It just happened?

I winced. "Point."

She ducked out of sight and stepped out a few moments later, wearing my sweats better than anyone had ever worn them. I pointedly didn't look at the way the shirt clung to her chest.

Domo had been right about one thing—Alysa and I were supposed to be enemies. Created in the lab of the famous Koschei the Deathless, Alysa was one of the most dangerous living artifacts in the world. Her ferret form was a portal to Vyraj that Koschei had created for his personal use. And me? Well, I was Baba Yaga's grandson. Yes, *the* Baba Yaga.

Matron of the forest, Bogeyman of the Slavic world, eater of spoiled princes, helper of noble knights, and an overall terror to all who crossed her. The only entity scarier than her is Veles, but then he rules the literal Slavic Underworld. Her daughter Dolya, the goddess of harvest and fate, had been my mother. Initially drawn together purely by circumstances, Alysa and I had nevertheless become friends over the years. Did I think she was hot, and funny, and smart? Absolutely. But I had always done my damnedest not to fall for someone who could go to Vyraj like popping into a grocery store.

"Look," I said to Alysa, fishing for resolve in my relaxed mood. "I can't do much about this. I can't leave my home undefended."

She scoffed, leaf-green eyes stern. "Can't or won't?"

"I'm just a harvest demi." I opened my arms. "I make good beer. All I can do is protect the people here. If I go out there, I'll get shredded. This portal opener might not even be — "

"What?" Her lip curled. "Your problem?"

"I didn't say that." My mellow was evaporating fast.

"You didn't have to."

I put the glass down. She didn't get it, she couldn't. I had friends, coworkers, and other very squishy, very flammable humans that I had to protect from what was waiting for me in Vyraj. The strawberry wine tasted sour on my tongue.

"I'll be upstairs," I said. "Come up if you feel like it."

I was halfway up the stairs, when her gentle voice tugged at me.

"It's been twelve years. Don't you think it's time to stop pretending you're just a human?"

I slammed the door to my basement harder than I had to.

Upstairs, my crappy mood was greeted by the uproar of my roommate's drunken party.

"My Russian brother!" James, my annoyingly handsome and talented roommate, gave me a beer-reeking smooch on the cheek. My oldest friend was the lead singer of a nu metal band called Overkyll, and his tall V-shaped body made me want to give up on chasing women entirely. What was the point if he was always around when I brought them home?

"I'm not technically Russian," I mumbled.

He ignored me. "How was the Dog?"

"Fine," I mumbled, deciding to leave out the drekavac attack and the inter-dimensional portal. One of the best things about James was that he lived in blissful ignorance of the supernatural. His arm went around my neck.

"Did you get the nerve to ask Kiki out?" he asked in a stage whisper. "Or did you sneak in here with that hot anime chick?" His cackle told me that he already knew I had. "Alysa, right?"

James and I had been friends since High School, but sometimes I wanted to throttle him.

"Yep," I said.

He slapped my chest. "Cosplayers, am I right?"

I made myself relax. Everything was fine. As always, the familiar noise of the party filled that empty spot in my chest. I was among friends, and everyone was safe. I nodded at Min-Ho, James' band mate, who gave me a lopsided grin. His guitar was slung over his shoulder, and his guyliner made him look like a K-Pop heartthrob. Not that I would tell him that unless I was looking for a swift kick in the nuts. For a pansexual, he was weirdly touchy about his pretty boy face.

"What's up Dimmy Dim!" he said in slightly accented English. His eyes flashed blue in the semi dark. An apple sucker stuck out of his mouth. Aside from being a lead guitar in James's band, Min-ho was also a dokkaebi royalty.

The Korean goblin came to the States to study medicine, but had strayed from the straight and narrow to become a straight-out party boy. I bet his posh parents were so proud of him. I know I am. "Where is your famed beer, my brother?"

Alysa chose that moment to saunter up to us wearing my sweatpants, and brushing out her wet blue hair with my comb.

"Oh," James said, his eyes on the pretty shifter. "Oh! Heeey, uh, Alysa."

Her eyes went to me. "Dmitry — " she started.

"I'm gonna go for a walk," I said quickly. "Headache, ya know?" I returned her look. "Better you stay inside and well... Stay inside." I didn't add "the wards" and I didn't have to. Her mouth in a sour line, she nodded. I slipped out the door.

Outside, the air was fresh. I knew I was being broody, and that I was being an asshole. Alysa was right. The portals opening all over the city were bad news. But what the hell was I supposed to do about it?

My boots kicking rocks, I stepped off my front lawn. The wards closed behind me with an electric whoosh. I started up the pavement. Just to clear my head, I told myself. Just to get in the kind of mood where I could actually enjoy James' weekly bash.

A neon yellow shirt was suddenly in my way, nearly blinding me in the street lights. Confused, I blinked up at the man wearing a Dodgers hat low over his brows. He looked familiar. A pin on his shirt was vaguely snail shaped. It flared in the light of the street lamps. I recognized him then. He was the guy who had watched us on the parking lot in front of the Dog. He touched his shell pin, and his acid-puke shirt sizzled with ember sparks. The fashion crime burned away to reveal the kind of fancy brown suit you'd expect to see at your grandpa's funeral. My vision tripled as two more, identical guys appeared standing next to his right and left shoulders.

"Dmitry Kozlov," they said in unison. "We are Agent Killian from the Spiral. You must come with us."

"Wait... What?" I croaked intelligently. "What do you want with me? Aren't you the guys that manage the pathways between the pantheons and stuff?"

The three of them smiled the same stiff bureaucratic smile. "Among other things."

"I haven't traveled to the pantheons in years," I said.

"Someone has been opening portals, and releasing monsters all over the state of Utah. This is a universal offense. You are currently harboring a suspect for this offense."

I shook my head. "I have no idea — "

The three of them took off their hats in a duplicated movement. Without the hat, I took a good look at their eyes. In the dark, they glowed pale silver, with a turning white swirl where the pupil should be. The world grew fuzzy around the edges, like someone had poured water on a spot of paint. They merged back together, and I, impossibly, merged with them and was being pulled along a tunnel in the fabric of reality.

"You will come with us," they said in their three-voice, "and you will help us apprehend Alysa Lapina."

4

My back pressed against the tomb-hard chair, I tapped my foot on the cold floor, and wondered why no one had bothered to change the batteries in the ancient clock that hung over Agent Killian's head. His clones sat on either side of me. Their shoulders didn't quite touch mine. What the hell did they think I was going to do, bolt? I didn't even know where I was. It smelled like mothballs. If I looked out the office window into the rest of the building, I could see elegant arches, modern laptops, and women wearing stilettos. Our interrogation room, however, was as firmly stuck in the 40's as Killian's double-breasted wool suit. When his nauseating space jump had landed us here, I had half expected him to offer me a cigarette. The clock hand finally moved. It was midnight. I got sick of the tense silence. Well, tense on my end. Killian had cosplayed a mannequin for the duration of the last thirty minutes.

I did my best to ignore the literal pain in my ass. They could've put down a cushion, or something.

"Don't you people have normal office hours?" I asked.

"The Universe is open 24/7," he said.

Did the mannequin just make a joke? I felt like a nervous school boy sitting in the principal's office, but I couldn't help it. I needed to get out of there. Every second I spent in this fish tank could send Alysa looking for me. Last thing I needed was her stepping outside Domo's wards. What if they held me here all night?

"I haven't been causing any trouble," I tried again. "I have, in fact, have been lying lower than low." That was the understatement of the year. Killian ignored me. All three of him. I tapped my foot. "Are we waiting for someone?"

"Just me," a voice said from the door.

I looked around, but didn't see anyone. The door shut and a chubby hand that wasn't connected to a body slapped a stack of files on the table in front of me. As if someone turned up the opacity in Photoshop, the rest of the man materialized. He was an overweight short man who looked just on the wrong side of fifty. His bushy gray eyebrows were raised in a friendly expression. A well-groomed beard was just long enough to conceal a weak chin. He wore a sharp blue suit with a flamingo shirt underneath. His stubby fingers were covered in golden rings. Most of them, I noticed, had ancient-looking golden coins where the gems were supposed to be. He slid his cushy ass onto a chair next to Killian.

"Neat trick," I said.

He smiled at me, his cheeks round and pink, reminding me of a mall Santa.

"Why thank you," he said affably. "I suppose being half ghost has its advantages."

I didn't ask him if it was the ghost of Christmas Present. I looked between him and Killian, eyebrows rising. They looked like an opening to a 'blank and blank walked into a bar' joke, but somehow, I didn't feel like laughing.

The round man flipped open his file. "So, Dmitry Dolyavich Kozlov of Vyraj. Your last name means 'goat', doesn't it?" He smiled amiably. "A demigod, son of Dolya the Goddess of Fate, grandson of Baba Yaga. Impressive family line, I would say."

Blood rushed from my face, and I felt cold all over. They knew exactly who I was. This was bad. Very, very bad. Agent Santa saw my reaction and smiled a little satisfied smile that made me want to punch him.

"I hope you didn't think to stay anonymous. We are the agency that issues permits to all the supernaturals, after all." He tapped a page that had my photo on it. "Says here that you've been hiding in the human realm for twelve years, and haven't gone home to claim your demigod status. Your powers are mostly dormant. You've been living a half-human life in Utah. Your grandmother," he flipped to another page, "received a permit for your relocation for the duration of four years, on the account of familial persecution."

"Meaning?" I said.

"Meaning, of course, that you have been living without a permit for..." He made a show of counting on his chubby fingers. "Eight years, Mr. Kozlov."

Pain throbbed in my temples. I hadn't known any of this. I decided to play the crime drama skeptic who 'knew his rights, damn it.'

"Why should I believe you?" I asked. "My grandmother sent me here to give me a chance at a life. She would've told me if my status expired."

"And when was the last time you spoke to Baba Yaga?" he asked with a smile.

I went from cold to hot. "I... haven't had the chance. Lately."

"Or," he said, his good humor as fake as his smile. "You haven't seen her in years, ignored all her messengers, and have been living the good life in Midgard—or Yav, as your pantheon would call it—warded with the help of a house spirit. Illegally, Mr. Kozlov. Part of your contract has a drop of your blood that allows us to track you."

I crossed my arms over my chest, and fought to wrangle my panic. "Who are you?"

He steepled his coin-laden fingers. "My name is Senior Agent Frónima. Demigod, son of Charon."

A son of the Greek ferryman for the dead. That explained the coins and his claims to be part ghost. I crossed my arms over my chest.

"Eight years, huh? Funny how you didn't seem to care until now," I said. "What do you want?"

His smile widened. "I'm glad we understand each other." Agent Killian's three faces chuckled with him, giving me the major willies. "We suspect that Ms. Alysa Lapina has been opening portals between Vyraj and Salt Lake City. We want her apprehended. You, Mr. Kozlov, will help us convince her to come peacefully."

"I don't know what you're talking about." I leaned back in my chair and put my hands behind my head. "Haven't seen her in years."

His smile stiffened. "Today, you were both seen at the site of a major tear between realities." He shook head. "Let's not waste time with lies. Why do you think you are sitting here now?"

"We've tracked her for months," Killian said in three voices. "This was the first time we could get a location on her. Now, she is gone. But you will lure her back."

I hid a smile. At least, my wards were working. "What's he supposed to be?" I whispered dramatically to Frónima and wiggled my eyebrows at Killian and his two clones. "Son of Cerberus?"

Frónima sighed like a patient grandpa. "Mr. Kozlov," he said. "I'd like you to understand the situation that you're in. If you don't help us bring in Ms. Lapina, there will be consequences."

"Alysa isn't the one opening portals. Besides, why can't you bring her in yourself?" I asked, eyes narrowed. "Like you said, you saw her just today."

For the first time, Frónima looked uncomfortable. Killian's three pairs of eyes flicked to his superior and back.

My eyebrows shot up in realization. "You can't catch her, can you?" Frónima gave me his best poker face and I laughed. "She's too fast for you."

"Dealing with a living portal can be difficult," he finally admitted. "She can move in and out of spaces freely, and there is no magic that can hold her. We are forced to recruit outside help."

A knock on the door made the Senior Agent look up. The door opened and an emaciated-looking secretary slid in on her stilettos.

"A call for you, Senior Agent," she chirped. "It's from the Intersect Committee. Urgent, sir."

Frónima sighed again and closed my file. He slid it into his blue jacket. A flash of gold caught my eyes as he straightened his collar. At first, I thought it was the coin rings. Then, I realized the golden glow was coming from his right palm.

"Thank you, Rachael." He turned back to me. "It's quite simple Mr. Kozlov. If you convince Ms. Lapina to let herself be taken into custody, your permit will be extended. You can go back to living your life."

My thoughts went back to the contract for the warehouse that just needed my signature.

"Alysa is not the opener," I said. "Someone else is doing it."

"That is for us to determine," he said. "You're not allowed to leave the city. And believe me when I say we can find you anywhere. Your cooperation is mandatory."

"And what if I don't turn her in?" I asked.

His belly nudging the edge of the table, Frónima rose from his seat. I already knew the answer, but it still felt like a cold bucket of what pouring over my head.

"You will be shipped bodily back to Vyraj." His eyes found mine and I saw that they were as dark and pitiless as the inside of a well. "I'm sure your family have missed you."

When Killian dragged me back through realities, it was only my pride that let me hold on to my dinner. I was two blocks from my house, near a neighborhood bank. Without another look at me, Killian blurred and was gone. That's a fine how-do-you-do. At least I had those fond memories of the time we spent together. I shivered in the early morning. They had found me too easily. If the spiral felt like it, they could throw me to the wolves that were my cousins. Some of them were literal wolves. Hands rubbing my arms, I started toward the house. How had the last twelve hours gone so wrong?

Hearing my name, I turned around. Min-Ho and James were walking up the street and their eyes promised murder. The goblin reached me first. He wore his band's leather jacket with the letter OK for "Overkyll" to ward off the morning's dewy chill. It looked warm and I was jealous. The sun was graying the horizon. It must've been at least four in the morning.

"What the hell, man?" Min-Ho demanded after giving me a quick once-over. "We looked for you for hours. I almost called the cops."

"That would've been helpful," I said sarcastically. "The Spiral took me."

He dark eyes widened. "What? Those universe-guarding spooks?"

"Yep." James caught up to us and I jerked my chin. "I'll tell you later."

My roommate's reaction was the opposite of Min-Ho's, and as always, predictable.

"Lover's quarrel?" he grinned and punched my arm. "Your cosplayer's been panicking all night."

"Something like that," I ground out through chattering teeth.

"Well." He grasped my shoulder in a manly half-hug. "I think you made your point, hot stuff."

At home, I went to the backyard where I found Alysa under a string of fairy lights. She had dark circles under her eyes. Her blue hair was pulled back into a ponytail and she smelled like my shampoo.

"What happened?" she asked. "I thought, maybe a portal, but the guys looked and—"

"I'm fine."

It took all of my sleep-deprived resolve not to grab her by the shoulders and scream "They're after you! Run! Run!" Instead, I shrugged as if I hadn't been abducted for two hours. I looked into her worried green eyes, and came to a decision. If I had thought about it hard enough, I would've realized that I made one already in the Spiral's interrogation room.

There was no way I was trusting that Frónima creep. Alysa was in my protection circle. Besides, no one told me what to do. Threatening me with deportation had been a mistake, Senior Agent. That left me only one option, and boy did it grate my cheese balls.

"I have some maps of the city," I said as casually as I could manage. "They're enchanted to find Vyraj creatures. Maybe they can help pinpoint the location of the latest portals."

Her mouth formed an 'O'. "Does that mean you're going to help me?"

"This better not take longer than a week," I said. Just saying it out-loud hurt my brain. "I have to sign for my warehouse next Thursday."

She squealed and threw her arms around my neck. Over her shoulder, I rubbed the bridge of my nose. Looked like Alysa was going to stick around for a while. Domo was going to kill me.

5

AFTER TYING THE STRINGS on my "Kiss the Chef" apron, I flipped the eggs in the pan. The biscuits were next and I propped the oven door open. The yeasty aroma of fresh dough mixed with the smell of grapes wafted in from the open window. I slid in the tray of the perfectly round beige circles. Domo's huge eyes peered up at me in accusation.

"What about my breakfast, master?" he whined. "I cooked for you."

I glanced at the burned omelette sitting on a bed of charred toast. Its droopy corners made it look like a troll loogie.

"I'm sure James will eat it!" I assured him. Sorry, roommie. "I'm cooking for two."

Domo sniffed and continued sweeping the floor with the thoroughness of a Roomba. He was a great housekeeper, but when it came to cooking, that was all me. James' TV was blasting news from the living room, and Domo had cleaned up after last night's party. It was almost as if Vyraj wasn't threatening to tear my home apart. Again.

Outside the window, my garden sprawled in its daylight glory. Lettuce, lacy and lush, surrounded rows and rows of cucumbers, ready for Domo's lacto-fermented pickles. Chilis, red as blood, and as spicy as Satan's ass, were almost ready to be picked. The entire backyard looked as if a green bomb had exploded in it. It was me. I was the bomb.

"Stunted powers my ass," I murmured, remembering Frónima's dig at my demigod station.

"What's that?" Alysa asked as she entered the kitchen and slid into a chair across from me.

"Nothing," I said. The coffee maker beeped and I poured us two cups. "Just happy to be here."

She eyed me over the mug I had handed her. "Yeah, okay."

In front of her there was a map of Salt Lake City. Years ago, I had commissioned a Gaelic fairy to enchant it for me. Now, it could show me all the monsters of the Slavic pantheon that were in the area. I had been fascinated with it the first few weeks, obsessing over seeing something that Golo could've sent—fire zmeis, or ovinniks, for example—but then grew bored with it. Salt Lake had a bit of ghost problem, and werewolves liked to prey on the occasional convention goer, but outside of forest and water spirits that could travel between pantheons freely, Slavic creatures weren't interested in boring, quiet Utah.

"There." Alysa tapped a finger on the map. "This is where the portal opened yesterday, near Salty Dog. And this is where the other two popped up in the last few days." She stabbed two red pins into the map and frowned. She fingered the one that was the furthest south, touching the city limits. "I think they started outside the city. It's as if they're zeroing in on something."

Cup in hand, I peered at the map. The Slavic creatures appeared as green dots. A lot of them were in clusters that dotted the city.

"Weird," I said. "Maybe the portals are just passing through. Like following a crack in the tectonic plate? But between realities? Is that a thing?"

She shook her head. "A crack between realities would act like a magnet. It would pull multiple pantheons, not just Vyraj. Why not Mictlan or Valhalla or others?" she said, referring to the Aztec underworld and the Norse hall of the dead. "That doesn't make sense. It has to be a person. Someone in Vyraj stirring trouble."

"Golo?" I asked.

"If he knew where you were, would he do this?" she asked.

I thought about it. "No," I admitted. "If he knew where I was, my house would be a pile of ashes."

Domo's bulging yellow eyes emerged from under the table.

"Here you are, honored guest," he said and placed a plate with a powdered donut in front of Alysa. The smile plastered on his grimy face could turn milk. "Please enjoy."

With a greasy giggle, he disappeared under a chair. She gave me puzzled look.

"I wouldn't eat that," I told her.

"Duuuuude," my roommate's voice came from the living room. "This is too weird, come take a look."

I placed the donut next to the burned omelette and went to see what had stirred up James.

A picture of a lake flashed on the screen, replaced by a concerned-looking reporter standing in front of a campsite. The tents behind him looked torn out of the ground by a storm. Or something as strong as a storm.

"Reports of animal attacks are being phoned in at an alarming rate. Following the decimation of the Dixie Creek campground, a Provo man is still missing and presumed dead. Anyone who has any information — "

James turned down the volume. "Apparently," he said, "we got bears this year or something. Someone also got half his calf chomped in the water and his canoe looks like something from the set of Jaws." His eyes went up to me. "Do we have barracudas in Utah?"

I didn't answer him, my eyes on the screen. A woman held a sobbing boy in front of a dead campfire. Their sleeping bags were dragged outside and torn, their cooler raided, their tent hanging in shreds. Just normal folks, having a normal camping trip. Until the monsters got the dad.

Alysa quietly approached and stood by my side. She and I exchanged a look.

My jaw twitched, and my fist curled. It would take weeks to hunt the monsters down. *If* the portals stopped appearing. No wonder the Spiral had their panties in a bunch. Alysa caught my eyes, her hand going to her throat. I read the same apprehension in her eyes that I felt tightening my chest. I rubbed my face, wishing I could just spend the day checking the maps and making some calls. Humans being picked off meant that I couldn't solve this problem from my kitchen. Which was too bad, because that was the extent of my expertise.

"Weird." My roommate's curly head shook from side to side. He ran his hand through his hair. "I smell breakfast."

My eyes glued to the screen, I nodded absently. "On the table."

James walked past me and Alysa and into the kitchen. I heard him rifling through the drawers, looking for a cup. I waited until he was distracted with coffee.

"We'll need an expert opinion," I said to Alysa. "Someone with a psychic sight. Do you know any friendly rusalkas?"

The operative word was "friendly." The water maidens of the Slavic pantheon were seers, but they were shy and wary of strangers. I really, really hoped Alysa knew one in the area.

"I do," she said slowly. "But she is not around right now. I think she might be traveling Europe."

I groaned and rubbed my face. This was a terrible idea, but I didn't see much choice. Very real lives of very real people, not to mention my peace and quiet, depended on us closing those portals and keeping them closed.

"I know one," I said, finally. "She isn't too far from that campsite on the news. But she isn't going to be happy to see me."

Alysa looked up at me. "Why not?"

Before I could answer, James' voice rang from the kitchen.

"Ooh, a donut!—" A groan and a gag. "Why the hell does it taste like sweaty socks?"

6

Alysa portaled us to the Twin Lakes Reservoir. I landed at an awkward run. My stomach roiled, but I was able to hold on to my biscuits, which is good thing under any circumstances. The blue ferret dropped down beside me. Her landing was a graceful contrast to mine as her paws sent a little puff of dust into the air. Blurring, the ferret transformed into a girl with a blue bun on top of her head. She wore hiking boots and shorts that showed off her shapely legs. I shifted the straps of my backpack and waited for her to catch up. Luckily, I brought all the essentials. Ya know, mostly beer.

The clear air of the Uintas and the green of the pines didn't set me at ease like they should have. Last time I was here, I was a major ass.

"What is her name?" Alysa said. "The rusalka?"

I took a sip from my water bottle and slid it inside my backpack. The afternoon sun was already baking the crown of my head.

"Katinka," I said.

"How do you know her?" she asked.

I hesitated. It was going to come up anyway. "We used to date," I admitted. "A long time ago."

Her eyes sparkled. "Didn't end well, I'm assuming." Her sly smile made me glance at her out of the corner of my eye. What was she so smug about?

"Not really, no," I said. "It was years ago, though, I'm sure it's water under the bridge."

"I'm sure," she said sarcastically.

"What's that supposed to mean?" I asked.

She shrugged. "You just seem like the type."

I stared at her blankly.

"You know," she said, "the type of guy that leaves a mess behind."

"Wow," I said. "Tell me how you really feel."

I'm not one of those Brodies that think women are a mystery. That's nonsense. I've never met a woman whose motivations weren't at least similar to mine. Everyone wants someone who accepts them, and makes them feel whole. Whether that means a one-night-stand or a marriage is dealer's choice. The bar for guys is embarrassingly low. All you have to do is not be an asshole. I had failed, catastrophically, at not being an asshole with Katinka. I mumbled something incomprehensible. Alysa waved it off.

"You're young," she said. "It's okay to be careless sometimes."

Bewildered, I looked at her freckled nose and rosy, glowing cheeks. "What are you, a grandma?"

Her smile was bittersweet. "Have you ever wondered how long I'd spent in Koschei's lab?"

I had to admit that I hadn't.

"I've lost years in ferret form," she continued. "I think Koschei kidnapped me in the 20's or 30's. Truth be told, I don't know how old I am. Every time I'm a ferret, time stands still for my human self." Her hand to her forehead, she peered at the sun. "We should take a break."

We found a shaded area on a bridge that stretched over swampy, green water. Being an hour away from the actual lake wasn't so bad. Sitting on the cool boards, I dug into my backpack. My palms grazed two dewy, cool bottles at the very top. I pulled them out and handed one to Alysa.

"Stumpy IPA," she read.

My chest puffed out. "The first IPA my brewery will produce. This is from the pilot batch." I couldn't help a wide a grin. The thought of starting my own—legitimate—brewing business, made the heat a little more bearable, and my feet less sore.

She twisted the top, took a sip, and grinned. "Veles eternal! This is fantastic." She took another, thirsty pull. "It's like a bitter citrus party in my mouth! And something else..."

A swell of pride threatened to make me blush like a school girl, and lose all my macho points.

"Blood orange extract," I said. "And a bit of godpower."

"Why "Stumpy?"" she asked.

I twisted my own bottle top off and inhaled the bitter goodness.

"That was the name of my tree house when I was a kid. It took me and the wood sprites six months to build it. It had a lot of stumps for support." I laughed at the memory of the awkward-looking structure. It looked more like a nest than a house. "That was the place I started making my first teas and wines." I shrugged. "Discovered the love of it, you know?"

"Back in Vyraj?" Alysa asked.

I nodded. "My grandmother didn't mind. It would be years until I could use my mother's needles. Back then, I was a little demigod of the harvest, with a secret tree house in the middle of Mavki Forest. Everything that caught my eye was an ingredient." I chuckled at the early experiments that made me gag.

Alysa propped her chin on her fist, her sage-colored eyes unreadable. "Is it still there?"

My throat tightened. I shook my head. "My cousin found it and burned it to the ground. The wood sprites told him my location." Seeing a flash of sympathy is her eyes, I shook my head. "It wasn't their fault. Creatures of Vyraj are all indentured to one of my cousins."

"Which cousin did it?" she asked.

"Golo, the demigod of bad luck." I said. "The arsonist of the Burning of Smyrna himself."

She stared at me. "That was him in the 20's?"

"Yeah." I tilted the bottle and watched the golden liquid bubble. "My oldest cousin Zloba was pissed that the Greco-Turkish war was over. Golo was cheering him up." I took a sip of my beer. "Fires are his favorite. His ovinniks burned it down."

"Ovinniks?" Alysa frowned. "I thought they only prowled human villages. They're not supposed to be violent."

I snorted. The black fae cats with fiery eyes and bad tempers were Golo's creatures. "If you don't feed them properly, they get quite an appetite. They will burn down anything with enough motivation."

Alysa frowned at her half-empty bottle. "I'm sorry, Dmitry."

I twisted the cap closed on my bottle. "It was a long time ago."

I hadn't told her all of it, of course. I had been nine years old. Golo had beaten the snot out of me, and tried to take my mother's needles. Of course, he couldn't, since they were bound to me. His fingers went right through them. He tried to make me offer them willingly, but I refused. That's when he tied me to a nearby tree and forced me to watch my sanctuary burn down. And that wasn't a story you tell on a bright summer afternoon.

Our beers finished, we found the hidden shack that I hadn't used in years. In the last five years it had grown into the hill and it took some prying to get the door open. Inside, a little red canoe sat in the corner. Alysa and I dragged it out and sat it on the shore of the lake. Luckily, it was still steady and leak-free even though I hadn't rowed it to Katinka's island in a while. The shifter couldn't portal us for another few hours. Taking someone besides herself through realities took too much energy, and she could get seriously hurt doing it.

"How long were you seeing this girl?" Alysa asked, wiping the sweat off her forehead.

"We dated for about a year and a half," I said and hopped into the canoe. Its bottom wobbled under my feet. Holding an oar, I stabbed it into the sand to hold it still while Alysa climbed in. I held out my hand and grasped her fingers to steady her. "I used to visit her here when she didn't feel like staying in the city." I didn't elaborate on how we'd spend summer days making love on the shores of the island. She'd been so beautiful, Katinka. From the moment I met her at the aquarium in the city, I had no chance. She'd smelled like pond lilies. Like home. "She'd spend half her time in Vyraj. The other half, with me." Like other water spirits, rusalkas can use the waterways to travel between pantheons. Unlike Alysa, they can only take themselves.

She took the second oar from the bottom of the canoe and blew a blue strand out of her eyes as she settled.

"I'm not going to ask what happened," she announced.

"Good," I said. "Because I'm not gonna tell you."

She huffed, and I grinned.

Katinka's island was twenty minutes away from the shore, if I rowed directly to the center of the lake. Its pines were amber in the sun, and the water sloshed against the sides of the canoe in gentle waves. The nose of the canoe glided up the pebbled shore. We staked the boat and walked up the slope. Dragonflies slid over the water, and daisies dotted the emerald grass. Alysa stretched her arms over her head.

"No wonder a rusalka lives here," she said. "This is almost as beautiful as Vyraj."

I nodded. "And no competition for the fish."

As if to contradict me, a dark shape slid under the water, right beneath the sparkling surface. A large shape.

"What was that?" I asked.

"Probably just the current," Alysa said.

When I looked back, the dark shape was gone. I breathed through uneasiness. I was too nervous for my own good. It'd probably been long enough that Katinka had forgiven me. Forgotten our fight, maybe?

I dug into my backpack and pulled out a block of Rice Krispies treats. Breaking the foil, I placed it down near the water.

"An offering?" Alysa guessed.

I nodded. "Rice Krispies are her favorite." Leaning over the reservoir, I dipped my fingertips into the clear water. "Rusalka, daughter of water," I murmured the summoning in

Old Slav that Katinka had taught me. "Heed my call, accept my gift, and tell me the secrets of the world." The words were simple, but they hummed with the ancient energy of Vyraj's magic. My needles vibrated in my pocket, responding with magic of their own. A gust of wind picked up my hair and sent ripples over the water.

"What if she doesn't show?" Alysa asked.

"Then, I'm out of ideas," I said and winked at her. "And we can go home and eat your delicious lavender muffins."

She rolled her eyes.

We waited as birds chirped in the trees and the water splashed against the shore. Minutes passed and my palms got sweatier. I had really liked this girl, and the way things ended between us was entirely my fault. All I had to do, I told myself, was charm her into helping us. I'd done it once, I could do it again.

A splash of water made my eyes track the waves. A blurred shape shot up and exploded in front of us, bathing us from head to toe. I leapt to my feet.

A girl stood in front of us, wearing a white, wet shift that clung to her body and wrapped around her legs. Her long blond hair draped over one shoulder, covering one breast. My mouth dried at the sight of her near-naked body. I clasped my backpack in front of myself as sexy memories crushed over me, and my blood rushed from my brain to *other* places. All my plans to be charming evaporated as a pair of cyan blue eyes blazed in anger as they took me in.

"Ehh..." I unglued my stare from things I was no longer privy to ogling. "Hi, Katinka..."

"How dare you, Dolyavich..." The water behind her seemed to pick up and repeated her words in a weird gurgle.

"Dolyavich, Dolyavich, Dolyavich." I've never heard Son of Dolya said quite so creepily. "How dare you summon me?"

7

AS IF IT HAD a life of its own, the rusalka's hair slithered over her shoulder to her waist. Her eyes left me and burrowed into Alysa. I thought it had been impossible for her to look more mad. I was wrong. Her blue eyes darkened to teal and her cheeks flushed in fury.

"Is this how you come to apologize?" she hissed. "By bringing along your new woman?"

I glanced back at Alysa. The shifter gave me the sweetest of smiles and gave me a "this is all you, bud" thumbs up. Thanks, *bud*. Even though I was a head taller than Katinka, if anyone could blast me dead with a glare, it was my ex-girlfriend.

I made myself lower my backpack-slash-shield.

"Katinka," I said. "It's so good to see you. You look amazing, uh... And it's been such a long time." Veles eternal, I was babbling. "This is my friend, Alysa."

"Oh," she said sarcastically. "You've come to apologize. Three years later. How sweet."

"I... Uh." I gathered my wits. Finding the portal opener depended on me facing my past mistakes. Even if they were so, so stupid, and Katinka looked so beautiful, and... I shook myself. "Katinka, I am so sorry about how I behaved. I was an ass."

She crossed her arms over her chest, for which I was grateful. The see-through shift over her breasts had been making my thoughts slam into each other like linemen.

"An "ass" doesn't even begin to cover it," she said.

"It doesn't," I agreed.

Her eyes darted between the treats and me.

"I behaved horribly," I said. "I went looking for you, you know, but—" Out of the corner of my eye, I saw Alysa shake her head. It was too late.

Katinka's white teeth flashed. "You should've looked harder! You should've never stopped!"

I raised my hands. "You're right. I know you're right and I should've tried harder to apologize." I picked up the Rice Krispies. "I brought you your favorite."

Her eyes darted between my apologetic face and the treats. She snatched them out of my hand. The foil rustled as she unwrapped it. In the sunlight, her skin shimmered as if it was covered with tiny scales. She possessed the kind of beauty that made men crash their cars, and I had been a fool to let her go.

"What do you want?" she asked. Her voice wasn't any gentler, but at least she was too busy with sugar to glare at me. "I know you. You wouldn't show up here after years just to apologize."

Ouch.

"Um..."

Alysa came to my rescue. "There are portals into Vyraj opening all over Utah."

Katinka humphed. "A blind fish could tell you that. One opened here just last week."

Alysa and I exchanged a glance.

"Did anything come out of it?" I asked.

Katinka shrugged. "How would I know?"

"Humans know that something is happening," I said. "It's all over the news. Something is attacking campers nearby."

"What do I care?" she said in the same tone.

"I don't need you to do anything," I said. "I just need your help finding out who is opening the portals."

Her eyes flicked to the water. After a contemplative chew, she swallowed a bite.

"And that's why you found me," she said sweetly, which was *so* much worse. "So I can read the universe for answers."

There was no going back and I nodded. "Yes. I should've come sooner. But, yes." I shifted from foot to foot. "You are the best at it, you know."

She looked suddenly cheered up. "I am, aren't I?" There was about half of the Rice Krispies left and she tucked the packet into the pocket of her gown. "Fine. For old times' sake."

She neared me and I could smell the pond lilies of my home. I tugged on my collar. Was it me or was it getting a little hot? Her hand touched my face and her eyes dilated, filling the blue of her irises with black. I gulped. That's what her eyes had looked like back in the day, when...

"The portal opener you seek," she whispered. "is veiled from me. Warded by fate, hidden by providence. You must seek Gamayun of Lukomorye, and she will have answers for you, for she can see through wards."

"Lukomorye?" I asked. It sounded familiar, but my brain was too scrambled to think clearly.

"An island off the coast of Vyraj," she whispered. "Where the World Tree's roots drink deep in Veles' Underworld, and its branches reach to heaven." Her mouth was so close to mine, I felt the heat of her breath. Small crumbs of sugar clung to her full upper lip. "Where all the worlds meet, you will find the Gamayun and ask her."

She stepped back and I could finally breathe. I looked back at Alysa and saw her stare back in alarm. The Gamayun was the half-maiden half-bird that spoke prophecy. No one has seen her in a hundred years. As if no longer interested in me, Katinka wandered down to the shore. Her feet sloshed water as she twirled, her arms spread out like wings.

"I can't go to Vyraj," I said to Alysa. "If I set foot in there, I'm dead meat."

She nodded. "I can talk to Gamayun myself. You'd just make a mess of things."

I made a face. "Yeah. I'm only good at diplomacy when there's beer involved. I'll stay here."

"Had to twist your arm, I see," she said with a smile.

"What can I say?" I spread out my arm. "I'm a pro at holding down the fort." I turned back to Katinka who had stopped spinning. She was now looking at us with a smirk on her face. "Thank you," I said to her. "Truly."

"You're welcome, Dolyavich," she answered. "Thank you for the offering."

"All is forgiven, then?" I asked.

She glanced at the water, and her smile broadened. "Yes, yes, forgiven," she said quickly. "I wish you a long, and happy life, demigod."

"You don't have to be so formal," I said. "I can come visit you—"

Her golden hair trailing after her like a tail, Katinka dove into the water. She disappeared beneath the waves with a neat splash.

"—sometime," I finished lamely.

Alysa tittered behind me. "Hitting on your ex? Classy."

"Come on, you saw her!" I said, defensive. "Besides, she forgave me, and told me something useful, that's more than you could do—"

Water exploded in front of us. A shape the size of a semi-truck barreled into the sky. Emerald scales and a maw full of shark teeth flashed past us as a water zmei, the bane of the Slavic seas, blocked out the sun. It looked at least five stories tall. Its tail sailed overhead and crashed into the water, creating a small tsunami that slammed into our canoe, swallowing it like a Tic Tac. A pair of white eyes bore into us and a screech that could've belonged to a T-Rex shook the trees.

"Did she, Dmitry?!" Alysa shrieked. "Did she forgive you?!"

Veles eternal. We were screwed.

8

ALYSA AND I CLUNG together like two chihuahuas at the sight of a pit bull. The zmei opened its maw and ejected a waterfall out of its mouth. Pushing off each other, we fell apart. Alysa stared at the two feet-deep water-filled crater in the place where we had just stood.

"What the hell," she panted, "did you do?"

"Ehh." I grabbed my needles from my back pocket. "I might've accused her of betraying me to Vyraj." The needles changed shape in my palms. "Then called her a treacherous asshole." I winced. "Then dumped her."

The shifter threw me a 'you've got to be kidding me' look.

The zmei's milky eyes were tracking our movement. I jumped up and down until its ugly, slimy head snapped to me.

"I thought she had, ok?" I yelled over my shoulder.

A single oar, the only thing left of our canoe, washed up ashore. Alysa snatched it and held it in front of her like a bo staff. The zmei's tail sailed over her head. She ducked inexpertly, tripping over her own feet. Alysa shrieked as the tail came back down with a flash of scales. The blow that followed made my shoes sink into the ground.

"Portal out!" I bellowed.

She scrambled up to her feet. "Like hell, I will!"

At least she had the sense to get behind me. "Can't you use your demigod powers?" she squeaked. "Send it back to Vyraj or something?"

"Great idea." I said sarcastically. "I'll get right on that."

Truthfully, I had no idea what my full powers were. Frónima was right. As soon as the needles recognized me, I should've returned to Vyraj. I had never claimed my powers. They sure would have come in handy now. Who knew that I would need to fight off anything bigger than garden fairies?

"Get away from the water," I said to Alysa as the zmei wound up for another round of projectile water vomit. "Shift and hide behind those boulders. If I need help, I'll call."

She nodded and sprinted off. Of course, I wouldn't be caught dead calling her back. But now, I could focus on the immediate—and giant—threat. I considered my un-godlike powers. My best chance was to try and blind it. My only chance, really. Throwing daggers at it would only piss it off.

Aiming at the zmei's ugly maw, I sent Veter sailing toward the beast's right eye. The dagger flew like a dart, razor sharp and fast as light. My aim was perfect, and my dagger true. But the best laid plans—

The zmei jerked its head and the blade sunk into its right nostril. The beast roared.

Shit.

Catching the golden thread that connected the daggers, I yanked. It was no use. My throw had been too good. Veter was lodged deep within the nose. I yanked again and was rewarded with a stinking shower for my efforts. The beast reared back, pulling my two feet in the air as it shrieked in pain. There was only one thing to do now. I'd have to go and get Veter myself.

I propelled myself along the thread that connected the daggers. The water blurred beneath me. When I landed on the zmei's head, my feet slipped out from under me. I fell on all fours. My balls barely missed the spiked ridge that protruded from its crown. Upside down, my hands wrapped around the ridge of its nose, I looked up into one milky eye.

"Hi," I said.

The beast roared and shook its head. Deafened, I held on for dear life. My palms dug into the azure scales. They were much sleeker than they looked. Eyes squeezed shut, I shoved a hand into the zmei's nostril. Good thing I was so terrified that I forgot to be disgusted. Hot, bloody snot covered my arm to the elbow. I grappled for Veter inside the cavernous nose. It took me a couple of tries until I found the slippery handle. I circled my fingers around the handle and yanked it out. The zmei screeched with the now-familiar T-Rexian pitch. With a mighty jerk of its gargantuan neck, the zmei hurled me into the air.

The shore dwarfed away from me. The water drew close, quicker than I thought possible. At the last second, I tried for a graceful dive. Instead, I belly-flopped like a toad on the pavement. I sank, water in my ears and nose.

Thrashing up to the surface, I gulped air. My limbs trembled and it hurt to breathe. Above me, the zmei snapped its jaw in my direction. Its tail crashed down. The resulting wave pushed me back beneath the surface.

In the depths, I saw a familiar glow. The portal to Vyraj that Katinka mentioned. That's how the zmei had gotten here. What else had gone through? Vyraj had a number of water spirits that liked snacking on humans. I needed to close it as soon as possible. Which meant getting past the zmei.

I kicked myself back up to the surface. Blinking water out of my eyes, I didn't see the zmei anywhere. I swirled in the water. It was just gone. We were half an acre from the shore, and I couldn't fathom where it could've gone. Then, it dawned on me. Duh. If it wasn't above water, there was only one place it could be.

I began paddling toward the shore. The theme music from Jaws played in my head as I swam like I had never swum before. Damn it, Katinka could've warned me. Of course, she didn't. I couldn't be sure she didn't call it. Rusalkas made great friends, but bitter enemies. And because I had been a paranoid idiot, I'd made her my enemy.

One night, feeling particularly mellow after sex and a bottle of pinot we had split between us, I confessed to her that I was the demigod the whole of Vyraj was looking for. She didn't seem to care, and suggested that we go visit home together. Swim in the streams. Pay a visit to Baba Yaga. I had agreed. The next day, a pair of ovinniks, Golo's creatures, had raided a neighborhood bookstore and set it on fire. I thought she had betrayed me to my cousin. I refused to listen to her explanations and ignored her tears. I had broken her heart. And now, I was swimming away from the biggest manifestation of watery revenge a rusalka could master.

I looked at the shore, and saw Alysa, her long blue hair tugged by the wind. Her eyes were wide as she held up the oar. She looked around wildly, looking for the threat. As if her oar would do anything against a freaking water Godzilla.

"Get back!" I yelled at her. "Go hide!"

My own panting loud in my water-logged ears, I looked around for a fin. Or something. A tail? The surface was still. Too still. Had it gone looking for a different prey?

I dove beneath the water and opened my eyes. At first, all I could see were specs of algae. Then, I wished I hadn't looked. A pale, snaking shape with an open jaw emerged out of the depths and headed for me. The IPA bubbled up to my throat. In its own element, the zmei managed to look even more terrifying. The shore was too far away. I'd never make it, I realized. I could feel the water pushing me down toward the predator, like a cork being sucked down a drain. I kicked my feet and my lungs burned. Welp, I thought, I had a good run. Dying because a beautiful woman was mad at me was pretty on-brand, if I thought about it.

A dark shape plummeted into the water above the zmei's head. It left a trail of bubbles that obscured any details. Sinking like a wrecking ball, it rocked the zmei on its path. The creature's muzzle broke its hyper focus on me and reared up to see the newcomer. Its tail curled around defensively as it turned to see behind itself, like a dog trying to get a flee off its back. I didn't wait for it to figure out what was wrong. Legs kicking, I swam upward.

The first gasp of air was like heaven to my abused lungs. I coughed, and almost sank again. I had spent too much strength in the water, and the fatigue that filled my limbs was dragging me down.

A hand grasped the collar of my shirt and hauled me upward. I smelled the rubber of an inflatable boat and a pair of almond-shaped, scarlet eyes glared down at me.

"Who, in Abnoba's name, are you?"

9

THE SUN-BAKED RUBBER BURNED my palms as I slid into the boat. Before I could take a better look at the stranger, I took my sweet time evacuating water from my lungs. When I was done, I slid to the bottom and stared up at my rescuer.

A young woman stared down at me. At first glance, she looked like a girl from South of the border—strong featured and striking, with deep set eyes and deep brown skin. Then, her appearance rippled as my god blood obediently stripped away the glamour. Beneath the illusion that fooled the muggles was a face not totally dissimilar. It was however, totally not human.

Dark ash skin replaced the soft brown, and her eyes flicked between maroon and burgundy, depending on how she tilted her head to the light. Tattooed lines ran down both her cheeks and merged into a line that disappeared under her chin. She was slender enough to look bird-boned, but her black tank top showed off lean muscle. Her black coarse hair fell around her face as she leaned over me, and that's when

I saw the crowning glory of her otherworldly appearance. A pair of honest-to-God pointy ears.

"Who are you?" she asked again. Her wide mouth twisted with annoyance. My mouth dropped open as I just stared at her ears. I had a suicidal impulse to touch them. She had an accent that sounded vaguely German. Crouching, she grabbed me by the front of my shirt. The strength of her grip was impressive.

"Are you deaf?" she demanded. "Or only stupid enough to swim in monster-infested waters?" She squinted at me. Her nostrils flared as she breathed in my scent. "You're not human."

Among the supernaturals of Yav, honesty is always the best policy. We're all paranoid as shit. To hide your origins is to invite suspicion. And suspicious magic users tend to throw fireballs first and ask questions later.

"Dmitry. Demigod." I croaked. "Are you a fairy?"

"Yes." She rolled her eyes in disgust. "A bloody fairy, that's what I am."

The zmei chose that moment to explode out of the water. Its teeth gleamed as its maw roared up to the sky. Its gigantic body sent huge wave after wave that rocked our rubber boat. I squinted against the sun, not understanding what I was seeing. The creature looked... Panicked.

A man rode the back of the zmei's head. His shoulders bulged, and his black hair trailed in the wind. His sword was brilliant in his grasp as he rode the zmei like it was his personal pony. The creature tried shaking him off, but had no luck. He'd lodged his thighs on the sides of the spine I'd almost lost my balls on. The zmei bucked, but the madman just rolled with the movement.

"Coria!" he bellowed from the top. "Now!"

She dropped me like a sack of turnips and grabbed a suitcase from the bottom of the boat. I watched, slack-jawed, as she flung it open. It was filled with rows of vials. She chose an empty one. The zmei rider yelled at her in a language that sounded like a mix of German and Latin to my ignorant ass. Coria—if that was her name—pulled the vial from its thong. She thrust it in the air.

"Senimon transmutet!"

The vial shone blue in her hand, and the color crept down her wrist. Then, it exploded down and out, covering everything in sight. A film of writhing blue phlegm spread over the girl, the boat, the water, the shore. I felt sticky with it, but it was mostly in my head. When the blue wave hit the zmei, it crawled up its body like parasitic blue mold. The black armored warrior pushed off the creature and dove toward the boat, the blade of his sword between his teeth like some action movie badass. The zmei shrunk and the blue wave seemed to pull it down and drag it across the water and toward us. The blue phlegm receded away from where the zmei's massive body used to occupy the lake and crawled up the rubber boat. The girl's fist shone again and she corked the bottle with a smirk. I blinked at the empty spot on the lake where the zmei used to be. What the hell just happened?

A massive breastplate smashed the bottom of the boat, rocking it. I looked down to see the huge man with dripping black hair and skin literally the color of slate climb in with the girl's help. He made the rubber boat groan and sit lower in the water.

"Eh, hi," I said to him.

A pair of equally crimson eyes measured me, and apparently found me wanting. He tilted his chin at the girl and asked her something in the same language he had yelled in before. She shrugged and answered in kind.

I tried again. "Thanks for the rescue."

He gave me a distasteful glare.

The girl sank back on her haunches, cradling the vial in her palm. "Don't mind him. He hates strangers," she said. "Well, he hates everyone, except me." She thrust her hand toward me. "I'm Coria." I reached over and grabbed her narrow, callused palm. She shook my hand, then nodded at her burly companion. "And this is Tynan. We are of the álfar. Dunkelelfen." she said. "The dark elves."

When Tynan paddled to the shore, Coria leapt out of the boat with liquid grace. She grabbed the suitcase hungrily and laid it out on the shore. The vials gleamed on black velvet, but she wasn't looking at them. Instead, she held the vial I'd seen to the light, looking at it like Gollum at the Ring. I moved next to her and looked over her shoulder. Inside the vial, a pea-sized copy of the zmei was suspended in water and baring its miniature shark teeth.

"So..." I decided to start with the thing that made the most sense. "You're dark elves."

Coria gave the bottle a little shake and squeed in delight. When she saw my puzzled expression, she grinned at me with a row of teeth that looked a bit too sharp.

"Do you know how hard it is to find a water monster this size?" she asked. "I don't suppose you have any more in this US state?"

"You're monster hunters?" I asked.

She nodded, her adoring eyes on the zmei. "Our tribe uses monsters in battle."

Her companion dragged the rubber boat ashore and began letting air out of it. Up close, his sword looked like it was forged of metal monster spines as the skeletal handle peeked over his shoulder. I had to admit that I was a little sore at the fact that he had taken down the zmei so easily. Who was supposed to have ridden that spiny hide and saved the day? Me. Instead, I flopped at the bottom of a boat like a fish. He didn't even seem to care that he taken down something so formidable, which somehow made it worse.

"This one will be a great help in the next battle," Coria continued. "As we face the island tribe Zugut."

"What pantheon are you from?" I asked.

Her red eyes finally broke away from the vial and landed on me.

"What pantheon are you from?" she asked. "I don't know enough about you."

I mulled over my answer for a moment, unsure how to sum it up. It was probably best not to mention the price on my head to a pair of hunters.

"I'm a harvest deity from Vyraj," I said.

"The Slavic pantheon, I think." She nodded. Then, her eyes narrowed. "And you just decided to go for swim? With a monster from your homeland."

"It's a little more complicated than that," I admitted. "We came here to—"

Shit! I whipped around. In all the excitement, I forgot about Alysa. The shore was empty of everything but rocks. Where was she? My feet squeaked in my wet sneakers as I jogged down the shore.

"Alysa, everything is okay!" I yelled at the pile of rocks she was supposed to hide behind. "You can come out now!" She didn't swim out to get me, did she?

My heart sank when I spotted half an oar buried into the sand. It was broken in half. Oh no.

"Alysa!" I yelled. Panic seized me as I checked the rocks. She was nowhere in sight. I made my way to the water, hopping on one foot, then the other, to take off my shoes. I reached for my shirt to drag it over my head, when I noticed something on the waves.

The current carried the other half of the broken oar. On top of it, her little paws paddling with all her might against the stream, was a soaking wet blue ferret. Her ears perking, she chirped at me.

"Oh, thank Veles," I exhaled and peeled off my shirt.

Swimming out, I offered her my shoulders. The shifter climbed off the broken oar and onto my back. She curled at the back of my neck, wet and trembling. Her nails scratched my skin as she held on.

Alysa riding my shoulders, I returned to the shore. She chirped and her muzzle pointed at the elves.

"It's okay," I said. "They're friends. I hope."

"Awe." Coria reached a finger toward that ferret to boop her nose. "Is this your pet?"

Alysa snapped at her finger.

"No," I said. "This is my friend. She's a shifter."

I offered her my hand and lowered the ferret onto a warm rock. She shook out her fur.

"I think I have something to dry you," I told her. "You can change back, you know. The zmei is gone."

She hopped up and down. Her chirping grew more desperate. Spinning in a circle, she rolled onto the sand. I frowned.

"What's wrong?" I asked.

Coria knelt in front of Alysa. Her hair fell forward as she leaned her elbows on her knees in thought. This time, she didn't try touching her.

"Oh," she murmured. "Abnoba's mercy." Her crimson irises flicked up to me. "She must've been in the water when the spell hit."

Apprehension prickled the back of my neck. "What does that mean?"

Coria's lips pressed together in regret. "She can't change back."

10

Alysa chirped in alarm, and I felt dread press against my chest.

"What do you mean," I asked, "she can't turn back?"

Coria shrugged, cat eyes apologetic. "The spell strips creatures down to their essence. Werewolves and other shifters are forced into their *gutus solis*, their soul shapes. She was far enough from the blast that she didn't get trapped in my vial. But..." She paused and my heart nearly dropped out of my ass.

"But what?" I asked. "Is this—" I couldn't get the words out.

Her concern lifted from Alysa to me. Eyebrows shooting up, she realized what I was getting at.

"Permanent?" she said. "Abnoba no! She's left free, which means that it will wear off."

My throat loosened a bit, but I still wasn't convinced. "How long?" I demanded.

She shrugged again. "A few days."

I gathered the ferret in my palms. Wet and trembling, she looked so vulnerable.

"Oh, Alysa," I whispered. "I'm so sorry."

Tynan strolled over to us. He gathered Coria's suitcase and spoke to her in their language. His head jerked toward the shore. The female elf nodded and began checking her supplies for departure.

"Oh, hell no." I stood up to my full height. Setting Alysa on my shoulder, I crossed my arms over my chest. "You're not going anywhere until she's back to normal."

"Or what?" Tynan spoke for the first time. Of course, his voice was deep and melodic. He had the same accent as Coria. "Puny demigod. You couldn't stop us from doing anything."

I bared my teeth at him and my needles buzzed in my pocket, feeling my anger. Who cared if he could take down a zmei? My foot slid out as I widened my stance. I bet he wasn't as fast as I was. My brain told me to be cautious, but everything else in my body just wanted to take this guy on.

"Are you sure about that?" I asked.

"Abnoba's mercy!" Coria threw up her arms. "Will everyone please calm down?" Her wide mouth frowned as she looked at Alysa. "I'm sorry, little one. I didn't mean for this to happen."

Alysa hissed at her.

"It shouldn't have happened," I said.

Coria stood up. "Can we talk this over?" She looked at me plaintively. "Preferably over a meal. I could eat an elk."

I stared up at Tynan but he seemed to have lost interest in me. I wondered at his relationship with Coria. If he was her boyfriend, he sure was an obedient one. Still sore from my failure with the zmei, I itched to test his metal. Alysa cooed in my ear. I covered her head with my palm.

"Fine," I said to Coria. "Let's get going."

She nodded and started toward the boat, Tynan following closely after her.

"Wait!" I called to them. Sighing, I stuffed my dry shirt into the backpack instead of putting it on. "We can't leave yet."

Coria looked back, confused.

With Tynan watching, I suppressed a whine. Just when I was getting warm, too.

"I have to close the portal," I said. "Or I won't be able to turn on the news for weeks."

We took the elves' ridiculously expensive-looking RV to the mouth of the canyon. Coria drove while Tynan sat on a couch on top of a bear rug, glaring at me and managing to dwarf the large space. Not to be outdone by him, I glared right back.

"Did you drive this thing all the way to Utah?" I asked, my eyes going over the sparkling kitchen, the wide-screen TV, and the brand-new wall couches.

"Yes," Coria said over her shoulder. "We fly in from Berlin. If we have cause to hunt in the United States, we usually buy a vehicle in New York and travel West."

I bounced up and down on the cushy seats. I didn't have a snail's trail of an idea of how much this thing cost, but it was definitely more than my down payment on the warehouse.

"Do they pay well at the monster bazaar or something?" I asked.

Tynan's glare never stopped as he answered.

"Our tribe is generous and wise in their financial dealings. What about yours?" he asked haughtily. "Can they not afford to give you a good life in Midgard?"

"Oh," I said. "I moved out of my mom's basement a long time ago, Tynni." The irritated flash in his eyes made me feel all warm and fuzzy inside. "I suppose you can call that being an adult. Not that you'd understand."

Coria snickered and Tynan's lip curled.

I was relieved to be out of the fancy box on wheels when we stopped at a Mexican restaurant. After giving Tynan a long, appreciative stare, the cute blond waitress sat us at a nice corner table. Stupid hot elf. His spine sword still peeked over his shoulder. Along with the illusion that morphed his features to be more human, he had managed to cover up the hilt. Coria still carried her suitcase like some mad professor. I supposed that if I had dozens of magical creatures at my disposal, I wouldn't leave them behind either.

The walls were painted a deep mustard and dotted with chili peppers, and the speakers were playing Mariachi music. It smelled like burned oil. I took off my backpack and placed it on the seat next to me. Alysa chirped inside.

The waitress brought out the corn chips and a bowl of salsa. She blushed deeply as she took our drink orders, her eyes glued to Tynan. When she scurried off, I took a chip from the plate and stuck it into the backpack. Alysa tugged it out of my fingers and I smiled at the crunching sound coming from the inside.

"So," I said to Coria. "What are you going to do about getting her back to normal?"

Coria sighed. "There isn't anything to do. In a few days, she'll return back to her human form."

I leaned my arms on the table. "Am I supposed to just trust you?"

Tynan's mouth pressed into a line. "We saved your life, demigod. You should—"

Coria raised her hand and spoke a short, cutting phrase in their tongue.

"What language is that?" I asked.

Tynan looked at me like I was the stupidest kindergartner in class.

"It's the language of our people, Feuerzunge."

"Fire—what?" I asked.

She repeated it, her tongue slow over the syllables. "It means "fire tongue". It comes from the Gauls that discovered the Old Ways in France and Germany."

I nodded in understanding. The Gauls were Celtic tribes that occupied much of Western Europe. Like the Slavs, they knew things that the Greco-Romans were threatened by and did their best to stomp out.

"After the fall of Europe, we took the Ways to our plane and ceased our involvement with the humans," she continued. "Isarno is our home."

"What's with the monsters?" I asked. "You said you used them in battle."

"There are tribes that would take our land," she explained. "Isarno is rich in volcanic soil. When they come for what is ours, we rain blood on our enemies. My tribe has been the best at catching monsters for generations."

"So, you're like Pokemon trainers?" I asked. At her uncomprehending look, I clarified. "You keep monsters and train them to fight?"

Coria exchanged a look with Tynan. Her smile grew wide and I noticed, for the first time, that her molars were pointy like a cat's.

"Not quite," she said.

The waitress returned for our orders.

I ordered the shrimp quesadilla, and tacos al pastor. The pork was for Alysa. The starry-eyed waitress waited patiently while Tynan stabbed his finger at various menu items. He settled on enchiladas. When Coria rattled off her order, the waitress' eyes widened a bit. I wondered where the scrawny elf would put it all.

"Are you?" I wiggled a finger between the elves. "Together?"

Coria's red eyes flicked to her companion. "What, Tynan?" She burst out laughing. Tynan sat in long-suffering silence as her mirth died down. "He's almost pretty enough, isn't he? No, demigod, my family is matrilineal. We only wed women. Tynan is my armiger. Weapon carrier and bodyguard." I heard fierce pride in her voice. "We've seen hundreds of battles together, and his family's honor is bound to mine. Together, we serve Abnoba, the goddess of the hunt."

Our food arrived and my stomach gave an excited growl. Before I dug into my own meal, I made sure to separate the pork from the al pastor tacos. Loading the meat onto a side plate, I lowered it into the backpack. The least I could do was keep Alysa happy.

Coria took a sip of her margarita and cringed.

"What did they mix into this," she grumbled. "Sewer water?"

"Allow me," I said and wrapped my hand around the base of the glass. There were few natural flavors in the mix, but I did my best to repair what I could. "Try it now."

She took another sip and her eyes widened. "Oh! Much improved. Slavic magic?"

"My magic," I said.

Her head titled as she regarded me. "What are you doing here, Dmitry? All the way in Utah? I've run into some Russian gods in other parts of the world, but never this far in the American West."

"It's a long story," I said. "The short version is that in order for me to stay here, Alysa and I need to find whoever opened the portal that let in the zmei."

Coria sipped her margarita. With the adjustments I made to the alcohol level, the tips of her ears were reddish. "And how is it going so far?"

I narrowed my eyes at her. My jaw clenched. So, the fact that I ate shit with the zmei didn't escape her notice. Tynan smiled a superior little smile. Frónima's words made an unwelcome visit to my memory. Dormant powers, living a half-human life in Utah, he'd said. So what? I crossed my arms over my chest, hoping my years of going to the gym were doing their thing.

"Not great," I ground out. "That's why we need to talk to a prophet bird in Vyraj, but thanks to you, Alysa has been ferreted for a week."

"Prophet bird?" Coria said.

"The Gamayun," I said. "She lives on the World Tree." I pulled out my phone, Googled it, and searched the image section. What I saw were fanciful, pretty—and pretty erotic—paintings of the half-woman half-bird. Why did humans have to make most mythical creatures sexy? Some things really aren't meant to be. I coughed and showed the search to Coria. "Alysa was going to talk to her and find out our next steps here in the human realm."

Coria dipped and ate a chip. "And now? What are you going to do?"

Tynan raised his eyebrows.

I squared my shoulders. "I'm going to talk to the Gamayun myself."

As soon as the words were out of my mouth, I realized what I had said, but there was no taking them back. Not with Tynan's judgy eyes on me.

"I'm going to negotiate with the prophet bird," I said as firmly as my panicked heart would allow me, "and figure this situation out." Veles eternal, what the hell was I doing?

Coria didn't seem to notice that my sense of personal safety took a fall on its ass in the face of machismo.

"What about your shifter?" she asked.

Oh, right. I couldn't go to Vyraj while Alysa was ferreted. I had to make sure Coria didn't skip town and leave her in that state forever.

"I suppose I need to—"

Ignoring me, Coria addressed Tynan in Fuere-whatever. The armiger shook his head in refusal. They began arguing and I used the opportunity to dig into my food. I wasn't as hungry as I had been half an hour ago, but I had to keep up my strength if I had to—gulp—go to Vyraj and negotiate with an ancient being. I couldn't wrap my brain around it. I hadn't been home in years, and had no idea how to find my way around anymore. And without Alysa's guidance, I'd be wandering around in the dark, stubbing my toes on murderous creatures. Not to mention that I couldn't just leave her in her ferret form. I had no idea what to do. The flavorful shrimp quesadilla tasted like carton in my mouth. This was happening too fast. But then, what choice did I have, really? I had to find the opener, and it's not like Alysa could use sign language to speak to the Gamayun. I was screwed, really and truly screwed—

"I think we've come to a decision that could satisfy both parties," Coria announced. Tynan's face told me that *she'd* come to a decision and strong-armed him into it. Which was fine by me. "We will join you on your quest to find the opener."

"You will?" I narrowed my eyes at her. "Why?"

"Oh, perhaps because today was the biggest catch we've had all year," she said and patted her suitcase. "There are bound to be more creatures before you find your opener. This way," she continued, "you can be satisfied that we stay long enough for your friend to turn back to her human form."

"I suppose," I said, unsure. This solved the immediate problem, but I didn't even know what Coria was doing with the monsters. Was she trading them like cards or something? Could they be some sort of inter-pantheon poachers? There were questions I didn't have answers to and I didn't like that. "I'll have to think about it—"

A golden glow blinded me on the left eye. It came from one of the tables. I squinted across the restaurant. A middle-aged guy sat across the way from me eating a plate of nachos. He looked totally normal except for the fact that he was wearing an old suit. At the foot of the canyon. In ninety degree weather. The blinding light had reflected from a golden pin on his chest. A pin the shape of a snail.

Shit.

They must've used my blood to follow me. And here I was, breaking my parole. Not to mention Alysa in my backpack.

"You know what?" I said quickly to Coria. "That's a great idea, let's go." I dug in my backpack and pulled out a hundred dollar bill. I pinned it with a plate in the middle of the table. "Now."

Coria frowned but I didn't let her question my sudden change of heart. The man saw me standing up, and began to rise from his seat. We'd have to pass by his table to get to the door. Who knew if he was like Killian and could just pull me through realities, backpack and all?

"To the bathroom," I whispered. "Quickly."

Tynan gave me a hard stare, and I glowered back.

"Unless you want us to deal with the Spiral."

The name had the effect I was hoping for. If they frequented the human realm through the Old Ways, they knew who the Spiral were. Tynan's dark face went bluish.

"The Spiral is here?" he asked. "Why would they be?"

I grabbed my backpack and slid from behind the table. When they didn't follow, I hissed at Coria:

"You want to catch monsters or not?"

She nodded and nudged Tynan to get moving.

With one eye on the Spiral agent, I shouldered them both toward the bathrooms. Just as we turned the corner to the back, I saw the agent dialing a number on his phone. Pushing the confused waitress out of the way, he ran toward us.

My shoulders slammed into the door of the men's room and I shoved the elves inside. If I wasn't piss-scared, stuffing Tynan into the single stall bathroom would've been hilarious. I bolted the door. Reaching into the backpack, I grabbed Alysa as gently as I could and pulled her out.

Looking into her round ferret eyes, I stroked her between the ears.

"I know this is sudden," I said. "But we need to go to Vyraj now."

Fists began hammering on the door.

"Dmitry Kozlov! By the order of the Spiral—"

Alysa chattered.

"Trust me," I pleaded with her. "I'll explain later."

She gave a chirp of agreement.

"Right," I said. "Everyone touch your hands to her."

Tynan's face was way too close to me, packed in as we were. "What are you doing demi—"

"Do it!" I said.

He and Coria touched a piece of her fur, and I gripped my backpack. Gods, it would've been nice if I'd had the foresight to bring another t-shirt. Thank gods I had more beer.

"Now," I whispered to the shifter.

The bathroom blurred in our vision as Alysa tore through the onion layers of reality.

11

Inter-pantheon travel induces slight nausea on the best of days. When a living portal drags three screaming people through the fabric of reality, the sensory overload turns tummy troubles into vomitpocalyspe. We landed in a field of sunflowers that somewhat buffered my fall. As soon as my knees struck the ground, I puked my quesadilla right on an upturned sunflower face.

Once my oh-so-manly purge was done, I fell back, my chest heaving. My stomach ached from the strain. The oily fragrance of crushed sunflowers closed around me, and the sweet air filled my lungs. Brown sunflower faces looked down at me, framed in fiery petals. Bees hummed in the air. I looked up at the azure sky that was tinged with pink. Veles eternal, I was back in Vyraj. I was home.

I heard the sounds of retching somewhere to my left, and turned my head to see a dark shape through the orange petals. To my satisfaction, Tynan was on all fours and paying tribute to the gods of inter-pantheon travel. I smirked. Where are your muscles now?

I looked up and saw Coria standing over me. She looked a little green, but unlike Tynan and I, she didn't seem to have thrown up her lunch. She slung her suitcase over one shoulder. Alysa perched on her other shoulder, muzzle in the air.

She shrugged at my envious look. "I grew up in my aunt's apothecary," she said and slapped her flat stomach. "She used me as a guinea pig from the time I was seven. Belly of steel."

Reaching down, she offered me her hand. It was long-fingered and strong. I grasped her wrist and hauled myself to my feet.

The sunflower field was a glowing sea of amber. A sooty-green forest framed it on all sides. The air felt electric as if charged with the same magic that seeped out of portals. Despite myself, I couldn't help a deep breath and a grin.

Coria scratched Alysa under the chin. She looked up at the pink-tinged sky, and her tattooed face grew slack-jawed. "It's beautiful here."

I ran my hand through my too-long hair. "It is."

"Any idea where we are?"

As it happened, I did. Kind of. We were on the eastern edge of Mavki Forest, and pretty darn far from the shore that would point us to Lukomorye. Truth be told, I wasn't entirely sure which shore we'd need to head to. Vyraj was surrounded by sea on all sides, and had more islands than fleas on a dog. Somewhere in the back of my mind, I had an itch that the island with the World Tree was off the southeast shore. At least we weren't that far. Hopefully.

"Right." I checked the sun overhead. It was nearing midday. "The best thing to do is to start walking."

Reaching to Coria, I offered my elbow to Alysa and she readily hopped off the elf's shoulder and onto mine. I resisted the urge to stick out my tongue. See? I can be mature.

"How long until you can portal again?" I asked the shifter.

"One chirp for a day."

Three chirps. Three days.

"What does that mean?" Coria asked as she walked alongside me.

"It means that she can safely portal us the day after tomorrow," I said. "Taking all three of us across like that uses a lot of energy. It's dangerous for her to do it again before her magic recharges."

As we pushed our way through the sunflower field and to the edge of the forest, my pulse thumped in my throat. The millisecond of joy that I'd felt in the field was replaced by the glaring, all-encompassing horror of what I had done.

Twelve years of peace. All the hard work I'd put into building a life in Yav. Thrown away because some god-powered asshole decided to make his reality-tearing my problem. I had a sudden urge to chew my nails like I had when I was a neurotic kid that was always looking over his shoulder. Also, the guilt. Oh, *the guilt*. If we went west, we could be in my grandmother's house by nightfall. She could give us guidance—and some dinner—without batting an eye. I wondered if she sensed my presence. The depth of my longing to see Baba Yaga deepened with every breath of the piney, fresh air.

As if hearing my thoughts, Alysa's nails scraped my clavicle.

"Hey!" I complained.

Her whiskers tickled as she gave me the smallest of bites on my earlobe. B*uckle up, buttercup.* I sighed.

"Yeah, I hear you." I covered her head with my palm. "Find the Gamayun and go home. In and out." I took a deep breath, feeling my nerves settle a bit. A little scouting operation in the land I knew like the back of my hand. How hard could it be? I was born and bred in this forest. "Nice and easy."

"I couldn't help but notice," Coria said as she caught up to me, "that you're a bit twitchy."

"Noticed that, huh?" I grumbled.

"This is your home, no?" she asked. "You must visit often." Her smile warmed as she looked at Alysa curled at the back of my neck. "With such a handy travel companion as this."

"Yeah, often," I said.

"You must have family here, demigod."

"Oh," I said meaningfully. "I do. Lots and lots of family."

When Golo, Vizg, Zloba, Zavi, and Kori weren't wreaking havoc in Eastern Europe, the Middle East, and Russia, they were chilling here, or in Veles' Underworld. Not that I've met my oldest cousins—the hulking demigod Zloba, and the twins Zavi and Kori—more than once. Zloba was the demi of anger, and spent most of his time in the Middle East convincing people to bash each other's heads in. Kori and Zavi were personifications of Greed and Envy. Casinos, cock fights, and drug deals were much more their speed than a summer visit to our babushka's. They were hundreds of years old and, unlike Golo and Vizg, who were closer in age, took no interest in me. A mercy I had failed to fully appreciate, no doubt.

"Will they welcome you?" Coria asked.

I laughed. "If they find out we're here, they'd welcome us alright," I said. "With a knife in the back."

The elf looked startled. "Oh?"

"My cousins and I..." I searched for words. How could I possibly describe the hatred that lay between us, the semi-dormant need of one eliminating the other? "Were made for different purposes."

Her eyes lit up with curiosity. "How so?"

"My mother was the goddess of good fate and rich harvest," I said. "Her name was Dolya. She's Baba Yaga's youngest. Her older sister, Likho the One-Eyed, was her opposite. Bad luck and chaos."

"What happened to them?" she asked.

"They crossed weapons in a final battle when I was a baby." I shrugged. "A big explosion followed. Nothing could be found of them. Except my mother's needles, that were passed down to me." I brushed my palm over the needles under my shirt lovingly. "Likho's children took over her work after she disappeared. They wreak chaos and destruction now. I was supposed to balance them out after my mother's death. But—"

"There are—"Coria counted on her fingers"—five of them?"

I nodded.

"And one of you," she continued. "Sounds like you have your work cut out for you."

I snorted, the homecoming joy in my chest shrinking to a hollow ache. "Nothing's cut out for me. I am outclassed and outnumbered. My grandmother sent me to the human world to keep me from being roasted alive. If they catch me, I am toast, and so is my life in Yav."

"So," Tynan's deep voice sounded behind me, making me start. I had almost forgotten he was there. "You're just hiding from your purpose. Like a craven."

I whirled on him, my teeth bared. Anger and exhaustion made for bad bedmates. "You try having a target on your back, elf boy." My hands were on my needles. "Try that on for a day, and there will be nothing left of you but a pair of toned calves."

His red eyes lit, ready for a fight, and I was more than ready to give him one.

"Is that a challenge?" he drawled.

"Tynni," I said and was pleased to see him twitch in anger at the nickname. "After the week I've had, I'd be delighted to kick your ass."

His teeth bared, Tynan's shoulders stiffened and he did that shifty thing that boxers do when they go from relaxed to battle-ready in one smooth movement. I rolled my shoulders forward, ready to defend myself. Alysa chattered into my ear in protest.

Coria stepped in between us, and turned on her armiger.

"Tynan." Her voice snapped with command. She followed up with a long string of worlds in Feuerzunge, and if Tynan didn't exactly look chastised, she had definitely taken the wind out of his fighting stance. She turned to me, and executed a small little bow, hand over fist. "You have our tribe's apologies."

Her sudden formality made me feel awkward. I dropped my hand from my needles.

"Eh, it's fine," I mumbled. Now, *I* felt chastised.

Coria's eyes shot at Tynan. "What Dmitry chooses for himself is none of our business. Our only business is the honor of the tribe, and you will not break it."

The dark elf dipped his head at me. "Apologies," he said stiffly.

I ignored him. After he called me a coward, he could stuff his apology up his ass.

When we started walking again, Coria stood a little closer to me so that Tynan couldn't overhear. "So many cousins that see you as a challenge," she said. "You must've suffered when you were a child," she said.

I was growing sick of everyone making judgments about my life. "It doesn't matter now," I said.

"We are a warrior tribe. I grew up with plenty of orphans. I know a boy who was treated like a plaything when I see one," she continued. She said it so gently that I almost didn't take offense. Almost.

"I'm no one's plaything," I said through my teeth. I didn't add "not anymore" but she seemed to have read it in my expression.

She smiled up at me and cocked her head. "No, you're not." Her eyes glowed a deep, volcanic orange. "Do your cousins know that?"

It took me about two hours to realize that despite my initial sureness, we were totally lost. The birches and pines stopped being distinct and familiar. Now, they blurred in my vision with sameness.

Tynan trudged through the underbrush with the stamina of a long-distance runner. I watched him, ground my teeth, and pushed my own aching feet forward. Then, I recognized a pile of rocks that we'd passed at least half an hour earlier. I stopped and dabbed my sweaty forehead. Peeking into my backpack, I found Alysa curled into a pretzel, dead asleep.

Her muzzle was turned sideways as she snuggled into her paws. Tiny fangs peeked out from under her whiskers. Lucky punk. I resisted the urge to scratch her on the noggin.

"Right," I said to Coria and Tynan who had stopped to look back at me. "I'm going to climb a tree and see which way to the sea."

I spotted a tall birch whose spotted, velvety bark promised to not skin my palms, and headed toward it. The first branch was the hardest, but as my body remembered the years of scaling Vyraj's green giants, it became easier to find my balance and pull my body up. Of course, my weight had doubled since I was fourteen. Luckily, the yoga classes Min-Ho made me take had kept me limber. As I climbed and climbed, my thighs began to burn. Straddling a branch, I looked down and saw that Coria and Tynan had shrunk to the size of cats. Suddenly, I felt giddy, like I did when I was a boy, scaling the trees around babushka's house. Just like back then, I felt unreachable. I was especially proud of myself for not flipping off Tynan.

I lay back on a branch and peered at the sky through the meshwork of branches. When I was a kid, I loved getting lost in the Mavki Forest. On the days when my cousins were too lazy to torment me, it even felt like an escape. I pulled my needles out and held them up to the light. They looked so ordinary against the fantastic pink sky. Just a pair of needles you find in an antique shop.

The day when they'd finally turned into daggers, I had resolved to go home.

I was eighteen, and working as a cook at a diner. In the middle of my shift, I was busy ripening the anemic tomatoes they'd brought in for salads. I felt my needles warm in the pocket of my jeans. Where I had expected a familiar slender shape, I felt an unfamiliar swell. I'd bolted before the server girls thought I was happy to see them. Outside, I found two perfectly shaped daggers. They fit into my palms as true as if they were made for me.

Thanks the gods for YouTube, because it took me months to find a knife throwing coach. For a year, I worked tirelessly until the daggers were an extension of me. Finally, I wrote a letter to my babushka, telling her that I was coming home. The pride at the needles finally recognizing me eclipsed all hesitation. I would accept my birthright and face Golo, and the rest of my cousins. After five long years, I was ready to go home.

That evening, I took a shortcut after the gym.

"Hey kid, you lost?"

I barely had time to turn around when three guys tackled me. Using the advantage of my skinny teenage body, I had wriggled out from under their grasping hands, and cocked my daggers. The first one came at me. I hesitated cutting him. He pressed me against the wall of the alleyway. I struggled, aiming my dagger at his heart, and then I saw Golo's face in my mind, his lip snarled in derision. I couldn't do it, I couldn't kill this man, and I couldn't fight him off. All the bravado I'd felt in the last year leaked out of me like the air out of a balloon poodle. The daggers shrank in my hands until they were needles again. The second guy's fist came soaring toward my head and left me limp on the asphalt. They took my wallet, the month's rent, and my brand-new sneakers. When I came to, the only thing left on me were my needles. The one thing they couldn't take. At home, I tore up the letter to Baba Yaga. I wasn't ready, and I never would be.

And here I was, back in Vyraj. Not ready, or prepared. Just a harvest demi that was good at brewing beer. I put my needles away and prepared to keep on climbing.

A buzzing filled my ears, and a grinning face popped into my vision. It looked like it was made of brown leather with grooves like tree bark. I squawked, and lost my grip. I fell, hard, onto the branch below. My chest hit the bough and knocked the air out of my lungs. I grappled for a hold. My foot caught a perch and my arms grabbed hold of the nearest stump. Panting, I looked at the newcomer.

Torn wings that resembled branches, glowing pin-prick eyes, and toothpick teeth told me exactly what I was looking at. A wood sprite. My face grew hot. We had been discovered. What had I expected? There wasn't a way we hadn't been spotted by the locals. Maybe he didn't know who I was.

"Dmitry Dolyavich, demigod of Vyraj," he announced with too much enthusiasm. So much for anonymity. "Grandfather Leshi welcomes you home, to-to-to!"

Leshi. Of course. The old trickster god of the forest was the reason why we were lost. He loved messing with travelers who made their way through the Mavki Forest.

"We're just passing through," I said, with as much dignity as I could muster. I was fully aware that I looked like an idiot, having almost fallen to my death at the sight of the creature the size of my fist. "If you could ask him to let us through to the shore, that would be great."

The sprite's dry laughter reminded me of two sticks rubbing together.

"What nonsense you speak of, Dolyavich!" It twirled in the air. "Grandfather Leshi demands your company for lunch! Hop to it, to-to-to!"

12

T̲HE WOOD SPRITE BUZZED its branchy wings as it led us down a twisty path. The sun had dipped over the horizon and the smell of pine cones intensified, as if the woods got even more "woody" the closer we drew to the den of the forest god. I watched the sprite, feelings swinging from nostalgia to dislike. When I was a child, those spirits were quick to befriend me. They were also quick to betray me to Vizg or Golo.

"Who is he?" Coria whispered. "This forest god?"

"Most days, a friend," I said. "Depends on his mood. He's the master of the woods and he likes to play tricks. No one passes without his say-so."

She frowned. "Does it mean we can't eat anything he offers?"

I raised my eyebrows at her. "What makes you say that?"

She shrugged. "Hospitality is a debt to be repaid. It's dangerous to partake of a feast in fae realms. Enchantment or entrapment are common tricks."

I laughed. "I think that with Slavs it's far more dangerous to say "no." You risk being stuffed against your will like a Christmas sausage."

She gave me a fanged smile. "Oh good, I could go for a sausage."

My own stomach was too full of nerves to think about food. The sprite buzzed to a halt in front of the young birch tree. He looked back at us, his beetle face alarmed. That was the only warning we got.

A huge brown shape crashed through the bushes and barreled toward us. I caught a glimpse of yellow canines and black marble eyes before I pushed Coria toward Tynan. Scrambling out of the way, I faced what I had already expected to face—a bear.

The tawny beast looked at least nine feet long. When it roared, the tops of the nearby trees shook. Its thick fur was covered in moss and grass, as if it'd grown from the woods itself. It stood on hind legs and sniffed the air in the direction of the elves. Then, its—his—polished coal eyes settled on me.

"Go!" I yelled to Tynan. Yanking my backpack off my back, I tossed it to Coria who caught in mid-air. "He's after me!"

Because why wouldn't he be, since everything else was?

I started running toward the line of trees ahead. Its breath heavy and raw, the monster pursued. My legs, tired from hours of walking, weren't my friends. Soon, I felt myself slow, and the bear caught up.

Shit.

Ducking to the side, I turned and faced it head-on. Sila and Veter were cocked in my hands. If I could just—

The swipe of a claw sent me flying three feet in the air. I landed on my side. My breath was knocked out of my lungs. Spittle burst through my lips as I tried to inhale. The bear was on me like an avalanche of fur and claws. By some shred of instinct, I scrambled out of the way before the nightmare of all teddy bears crushed me to death. My torso twisted and pulled my legs under me. I saw a furry flank and drove Sila into it. The bear roared and his paws swept toward my head. I danced out of the way. My chest felt like it was going to explode and my vision swam with the shortness of breath. I kicked the bear right in the knife wound. He roared and fell back in a heap of muscle and fat. There was so much of him, it almost looked like he fell in slow motion.

"Timber!" I breathed.

I jumped on top of him, knees driving his paws apart. The point of Veter pressed under his foul-smelling jaw. I panted, looking into his glistening eyes. The space around us froze as we stared at each other.

The bear huffed, then chuffed. Then, he laughed.

"Pha-ha-ha!" His maw stretched in a freakishly human smile. I was too stunned to react as its paws broke through my hold and went around me. He rolled up to his haunches and I rolled off his belly.

"Dmitry Dolyavich!" he said in old Slav. "Oh-ha-ha!" He pulled us both to our feet—paws?—and steadied me. "That was amusing!"

The dish-like slope of his nose furrowed, and then his lips pulled back into a two-fanged snarl. A smile, I corrected myself. That was the smile of a creature really enjoying my shock.

The bear grinned wider and his shape blurred. Claws pulled back into fuzzy sleeves and the bottom lip reshaped and spouted a beard that fell down to his chest. In seconds, the bear in front of me was replaced by a gray-haired man in a bearskin coat. His eyebrows were so thick they draped down his temples. A pair of antlers topped his head. His smile crinkled his yellow, glowing eyes that reminded me of a wolf watching his prey from the bushes.

"Yaga's grandson." Leshi's heavy hand fell on my shoulder. "Welcome home, my lad!"

It took some time to convince Tynan not to pick a fight with the father of the forest. By the time the elves caught up to us, the armiger had wielded his spine sword and was filled with blood lust. For her part, Coria laughed when she heard what happened, and eyed the old trickster god appreciatively.

"A bear, huh?" she asked me. "He looked big enough for my vial collection."

"Don't even think about it," I said.

"What?" She grinned. "I'm just—what do you Americans call it?—window shopping."

She handed me my backpack. I opened it and found a very ruffled, very pissed ferret. Her chirping spoke volumes about how I'd be a dead man if she was in her human form.

"I know," I said to her. "I'm sorry. Come on, don't be mad." I reached inside. Her teeth sank into my finger and I yelped. "Ouch! Damn it!"

Coria snickered. With an indignant huff, Alysa leaped out of my bag, scrambled over my arm and hopped onto the elf's shoulder. Coria looked delighted and I suppressed a jolt of jealousy. Fine.

"What do you do with them, anyway? The monsters?" I asked, starting to follow Leshi as he waved us on through the woods. "You never explained."

"I'm a transmute," she said, as if that was supposed to make perfect sense.

"What does that mean?" I asked.

She swept her coarse black hair away from her forehead and tied it into a ponytail. Her smile was mild. "It's a secret of my tribe. Maybe I will show you sometime."

There was no time to press her as Leshi came back to pull me into—you guessed it—a bear hug. His arms around my shoulder, he pushed me toward a glade. I wasn't surprised to see that his limp had already disappeared. It was a miracle I nicked him at all.

"It's been such a long time since I had a satisfying bout!" he exclaimed. His yellow eyes twinkled as he wagged his finger at me. "You almost had me there, boy!"

"Why the theatrics?" I asked.

"Your purpose is to become a great warrior, like your mother!" His fingers dug into my shoulder like he was testing roast beef. "I had to test your merit for myself!" He released me and rubbed his palms together. "Here we are! Only the finest for Yaga's grandson."

A lush, patterned carpet greeted us. It was spread out over the grass. Plates of food dotted the fabric—bread, honey, roasted fowl, apples, a steaming pot of borscht, meat pies, pitchers of milk and beer. The carpet lay between several stumps buffed down for sitting.

"Please!" He opened his arms toward the feast on the grass, and beamed at my stunned companions. "Eat! Drink!"

We did so with gusto.

My appetite returning, I wolfed down pelmeni with sour cream, and chased it with the cranberry compote. The fatty dumplings went down like a dream, their freshness incomparable to what I could get my hands on at the Russian grocery stores in Salt Lake. Coria got her hands on half a chicken and ate it with such savagery I couldn't help but laugh. Alysa perched on Leshi's hairy shoulder and was nibbling on a slice of kielbasa.

"So," Leshi asked, his eyes lighting with humor as Tynan tried to suppress a cough after a careful sip of vodka. "Who are your foreign friends?"

"They're elves."

I told him about the zmei, and the portals that were popping open all over the state. Leshi humphed, and poured beer for both of us.

"A serious problem, indeed," he grumbled. "So this is not a social visit. You must find answers. Will you go to your babushka? She could help."

At his words, my beer didn't taste as delicious as I'd hoped.

"I don't have time for a visit. I have to find the Gamayun. She will have answers for me."

That wasn't the real reason, and Leshi knew it as well as I. The truth was that after all these years, I was too ashamed to show up on her doorstep. The forest god guessed what I left unsaid.

"Gamayun is dangerous," he said. "She was imprisoned on the island by Baba Yaga herself. You risk your own life, and your friends', for your pride." He waited for me to say something, and added gently when I didn't: "Gods live a long time. For you, it has been years in the mortal realm. But for her, it was but a blink of an eye."

I lowered my eyes at the foam on the sides of the beer mug. "What would I even say?"

"You could start with giving her a hug," he said. "You're her only connection to her dearest Dolya, after all. She will accept you, boy."

Running my fingers through my hair, I shook my head. "I have to make sure my home is safe. And my friends. Every moment I lose, Salt Lake is being filled with monsters."

"You really care about this," Leshi smacked his lips, "Sol Lek, eh?"

I smiled. "I do."

"Lukomorye isn't a place one can just find," he continued. "It requires intent that you lack."

Bristling, I scowled at the forest god. "How do I lack intent?"

He wiped the foam off his dangling mustache. "You're not bound to your power, young Dmitry," he explained. "You are grown now, and your needles recognize you, but your attention is scattered, like a newborn pup's. You must spill your blood and say the words of binding, as your grandmother taught you. Only then will you receive the whole of your mother's might."

The simple spell my grandmother had made me memorize surfaced in my mind.

Blood to earth, earth to blood, let my bond make me god.

"If I bind myself," I said, "I will be required to protect Yav from my cousins."

"Even so." Leshi nodded.

Shifting uncomfortably, I poured myself more beer. With a neat hop, Alysa jumped off Leshi's bear coat and landed on my shoulder. She draped her body around my neck and her tail tickled the hollow of my throat. Her forgiveness made me feel a couple ounces better. I gave her a rub under her chin.

"I can barely protect my home," I said. "Let alone the human world."

"For now," he admitted. "Who's to say what would happen if you embraced your mother's legacy?"

We were interrupted by Coria's roar as she draped her arm around Tynan's neck and sang something in elven. Wine spilling over the rim of her glass, she swayed from side to side.

"Ga!" Leshi barked. "This one I like very much!"

He joined her with a song of his own, and the two of them lifted a bleary-eyed Tynan to his feet. Feuerzunge and Old Slav made for a bewildering cacophony. Shaking my head, I climbed to my feet and clapped as they wailed up to the sky.

When the drunk elves were snoozing on a sleeping bag, Leshi beckoned to me. The sprites darted through the air, carrying plates of leftovers and empty cups. I was a little sauced myself, even if I tried to go easy on the beer. I perched on a stump across from Leshi, a little unsteady on my ass. There were crumbs in his beard. His grin doubled in my vision.

"I will help you find Lukomorye," he said. He palm opened and I saw a glistening ball of thread. "This will show you the way. The thread is made of the fabric of Vyraj itself. It is unbreakable and will lead you true. All you have to do is tell it the name of your destination, or person, you're trying to find."

I stared at the ball. Multicolored shimmers reminded me of a portal. "Thank you." I reached for it.

"Ah-ah!" Leshi held it out of my reach. "A riddle first." He smiled through his beard. "What happens when you don't go after a bear in the forest?"

I hiccuped. Couldn't he have asked me his riddle three beers ago? "You go home?"

The trickster god shook his head. His yellow eyes glimmered with specks of emerald. "The bear," he placed the glistening ball on my palm, "goes after you."

13

IN THE MORNING, LESHI was gone. Along with him, the remnants of the feast had disappeared completely. The only thing left was Coria's raging hangover.

"Achh..." She pressed a bottle of beer to her forehead. Luckily, I had a straggler at the bottom of my backpack.

"Better drink it," I advised.

Her red-rimmed eyes narrowed on me. "How are you so chipper?"

I shrugged. "I don't get hangovers."

Eyebrows drawing together in sympathy, Tynan twisted the bottle cap and let Coria sip the beer. His giant sword was back in its scabbard and peeked over his left shoulder.

"We'll find water," I promised. Alysa yawned and stretched on my shoulder. I felt sticky and gross. A scrub down sounded amazing.

By the time the sun rose higher in the sky, we had bathed in and drunk from a stream. I changed my shirt to the only clean one I had left and rinsed my sweat-soaked one. Once, I heard a buzz of twiggy wings. When I turned around, a loaf of bread was sitting on a stump. A wheel of cheese was next to it. Good ole grandpa Leshi. We shared the food and filled our water bottles.

I pulled Leshi's gift out of my pocket and admired the glistening threads that reflected off the surface of my palm. I fingered one multi-hued thread and felt the ethereal, silky fibers under my touch. It looked too delicate to be unbreakable. A part of me wanted to pull out the needles from my pocket and see if I could knit something with them, even though I've never knitted a thing in my life. It would probably waste the thread. Still, the desire thrummed through me.

"What is that?" Coria asked, a cold compress made out of Tynan's shirt pressed to the back of her neck. "Magic?"

"Oh yes," I said. "Very old Vyraj magic."

"How does it work?" she said.

I shrugged. "Guess we'll find out."

Releasing the ball, I let it drop to the ground. "Lukomorye," I said, feeling a bit silly. "Find Lukomorye."

Even though I was expecting it—Leshi wouldn't give me a dud—I still jumped a bit when the ball of thread began to roll.

"Well," I said, "there you have it. Let's go."

My legs still aching from yesterday's trek—not to mention my scuffle with Leshi—I expected my sore body to take a beating. I was wrong. The trees thinned around us, and within forty minutes the fine forest grass was replaced with bald spots of white sand.

Seagulls screeched over our heads. The iodine smell of the sea filled my nostrils. Soon, the trees ended altogether and the sea spread before us like a rippling silver mirror. We found ourselves on a rocky lip that hung over the glistening white sand of the sea. The ball of thread came to a stop and I stuffed it back in my pocket.

Walking toward the edge of a shallow cliff, I examined the drop. It didn't look steeper than nine feet. I didn't wait for Tynan to leap off it like an Olympic champion just to annoy me. Pulling out Veter, I aimed at a stump near the water. When Veter sat firmly in the wood, I followed with Sila. To the elves, it looked like I effortlessly materialized on the shore below. Sand splashed beneath my sneakers and Alysa squealed in delight.

"Wow," Coria said after she scrambled down the stoneface like a spider monkey. "Very impressive." Tynan humphed behind her which made my day. "Do you ever miss a throw?"

I shook my head. "Not really." This time, I wasn't boasting. Sometimes my supernaturally good aim didn't feel deserved. Not that I wouldn't take what I could get in a world that crawled with creatures who were bigger—and meaner—than me. "Unless the target is moving, almost never."

I breathed in the fresh, humid air of the sea. Alysa's muzzle lifted and she closed her eyes in pleasure as the breeze threaded her whiskers. The waves crashed against the shore. White foam bubbled and the wind picked up my hair. I immediately regretted not bringing a coat as the cold bit me.

In front of us, barely visible in the foggy distance, lay an island. Its rocky shore looked unapproachable. Even from a distance, I could see a tree that could be nothing else but *the* Tree. It dwarfed the island with its branches that reached out and up into the clouds. Maybe it was a trick of the light, or the distance, but I couldn't tell for sure where the crown of the World Tree ended and the sky began.

Coria came alongside me and eyed the waves with professional interest. Her dark hair snagged in the wind and her crimson eyes squinted at the distant shore.

"How are we getting across, demigod?" she asked. "Our boat is in the RV."

That was an excellent question. I began walking the length of the shore, looking for any sign of travel. There had to be a way to cross to Lukomorye, right?

The cliff curved and my eyes caught something out of place. A loose end of a rope. I walked towards it and saw that it cascaded down the stoneface. Following it up, I found the source of it and walked around a cluster of rocks that hid it from my view.

Bingo.

A thick rope stretched from the lip of the cliff and disappeared toward the island. Beneath it, rocking on the waves, sat a tub boat. It was connected to the rope above with a pulley. Another length of rope fell into the boat, implying that one had to pull the rope to drag it along the water to the island. It seemed like a long way for such a flimsy-looking vessel. I walked to it and rattled my knuckles on its sides. It was the size of a hot tub, and looked sturdy enough. Presumably, it had taken a few trips across to the Tree and come back safely. Right?

"It doesn't look very safe," Coria said when she caught up to me.

I cocked an eyebrow at her. "What about this whole adventure tickled you as "safe?"

"True."

"You can stay here, and I can go myself," I said. "You don't need to talk to the Gamayun. And it is safer on the shore."

She snorted. "Absolutely not. I'm not missing a good look at the World Tree. Do you know how hard it is to access in the fae realms? Stone giants guard it and a river of poison surrounds it on all sides. This seems like a boon from the gods."

I looked at the clear sky and the mellow breeze that gently pushed the waves. It definitely did. The whole idyllic display set my nerves on edge.

I turned my head to Alysa. "Stay in the backpack, okay? It's buoyant."

We piled into the boat. The process of Tynan squeezing himself into it without tilting it over deserved its own whole comedy skit. In the end, we were more or less comfortable, if slightly too cozy.

Tynan and I took turns pulling us across. The weather held and the first part of the journey was as peaceful as our launch had promised. The island neared as we drew closer to the mid-point.

Coria bent over the edge, her hand trailing in the water. Her suitcase sat on the curved bench next to her. It was my turn to pull and my palms were starting to feel the burn.

"This is boring," she complained. "I think it would be faster to swim."

I scoffed. "You're welcome to try it."

She rolled her eyes and splashed water at me. Tynan snickered. This was going much more smoothly than I had expected. Not a cloud in the sky, and not a wave too strong. Maybe we could go to the Gamayun, ask some questions, and be back on land in time for Leshi's dinner.

A cry overhead jerked me out of my meditative rope pulling. Looking up, I saw a bird. Then another and another. I shielded my face against the sun and took a better look at them. Their tails were long and their legs curved more like a lion's than a falcon's. I couldn't tell from the distance, but the breadth of their wingspan looked far too wide. Then, one dove closer. Its cry echoed over the water.

Anxiety gripped my spine. "Those aren't birds," I said.

Long hair whipping in the wind, the creature had a woman's head and blood-red wings. Its friends dove in and out of the clouds. They echoed the call of their companion. Wait, clouds? Where did those come from?

Coria looked up and Tynan reached for his scabbard.

"What are they?" Coria asked.

I wracked my brain. Alysa would know for sure, but I hazarded a guess.

"I think they're sirins. Maidens with the body of a bird," I said.

"Like the Gamayun?" she asked.

I shook my head. "That's like comparing lions to a sphinx. They're similar, yes, but the Gamayun is older. I think she's their mother, and mistress or something."

Tynan wasn't interested in what they were. He bared his perfect teeth. The metal spine glinted as he brandished his sword.

"Are they going to attack?"

I shrugged. "I don't know. They look like they're waiting for something."

Coria tapped her tattooed lower lip. She threw a glance at Tynan as if he held her copy of Monster Encyclopedia.

"Sirins... sirins," she murmured. "Don't they control the weather?"

My eyes darted between the bird maidens and the clouds that seemed to have come out of nowhere. More gathered at the edges of the sky. My clear day no longer looked so clear.

Lightning struck and the wind picked up like it had finally released its breath.

"Oh. Oh, shit," I said. Water thudded against the boat that seemed a lot more flimsy now than five minutes ago. I whirled to Tynan and threw him the end of the rope I was holding. The wind roared in my ears and the quickening waves splashed salt at my face. "Pull!"

Joining forces with me, Tynan pulled with all his might. The boat wobbled on the waves. The tub was propelled forward faster than it had been before, but the force of the storm made the rope above our heads creak. We bobbed like kids playing on a seesaw.

A wave crashed over us. My head snapped up and down as I gasped for breath. Alysa's panicked screech came from the backpack and I was glad I'd had the foresight to buy the kind with plenty of float. The sea was bitter in my mouth. Tynan was on his knees as his hands pulled the rope behind me. My own muscles began to seize as my grasp turned desperate. The clouds were so dense and black, I couldn't see the skies, or the sirins.

When we got a moment of reprieve, I saw the island wobble in front of us. I could see the details of the rocky shore. Well, the island didn't wobble, we did. Seagulls screeched overhead. We were closer than I had expected. Not that it would matter, I thought, as another wave consumed the tiny boat. The rope creaked again. It was trembling in the wind, taut between the storm and our weight in the boat. Tynan, his teeth bared at the onslaught of the water, pulled the rope with all his might.

"No-o-o!" I cried.

It was too late.

With a snap like a gunshot, the rope that held the boat broke.

The wind tossed us freely. The tub boat spun like a cork in a drain. We were as dead as a doorknob, I realized. Dead as nails. Unless I did something.

The rocky shore drew further away. Shielding my eyes from the salt water, I peered at it. An oak tree had found a perch between the rocks. Its fat trunk and green foliage told me it was healthy and strong. A mad idea dragged through my salt-soaked brain.

I thrust my hand into my pocket, and pulled out Leshi's ball of thread. My needles were hot in my hands as I pressed them between my teeth and began unwinding the glistening thread.

"What are you doing?" Coria screamed over the wind.

I didn't answer, cause you know, needles in my mouth, our lives on the line. With numb fingers, I caught an end of the thread. I began to wind it around the wheel mechanism that had held the pulley rope. I pulled the needles out of my mouth and willed them to turn into daggers.

"Help me!" I called over my shoulder.

Coria's small, powerful hands joined mine. She seemed to clue into what I was trying to do. Together, we wound and tied and secured until we had no more time. Using the leftover tail of the rope, I secured the hilt of Sila, using the criss-crossed pattern that I had learned in Boy Scouts. Once the power dagger and the boat were bound together, I braced my knees to the edge of the madly jerking boat.

The waves aimed to knock me down. Through the roar of the wind and waves, I cocked Veter in my right hand.

Coria's arms wound around my waist to steady me. "How about that moving target?" she yelled into my back. "Can you make it?"

"Just hold on to the boat!" I yelled back. I wasn't sure who to pray to for such a far-reaching shot. So, instead I said, "Fuck it."

I let Veter fly.

It pierced the air with a whistle, defying the wind, and the waves and every element doing its damnedest to kill us. Like a silver bullet it pummeled toward its destination. The magical thread hummed is it pulled through my hand. It stretched through the water like a glistening umbilical cord. I felt, more than saw, when Veter connected with the ancient oak. *Dolya's needles*, I thought, *don't fail your heir now*. Sliding back, I touched Sila and connected the daggers.

The boat stilled, then jerked. The wood creaked and we were flying forward. I was pushed into Coria who was pushed into Tynan. Clutching the backpack with the screeching Alysa to my chest, I barely had time to get bare-ass-scared as the boat whooshed toward the shore.

The parting waves slammed against us, and I was blinded. When the wall of water cleared, I saw that we had another thing to worry about. The rocky shore of Lukomorye loomed ahead, and every second pulled us closer to a crash. The bottom of the tub boat groaned.

"Jump!" I yelled at my companions.

We splashed into the water like wet puppies. Rid of our weight, the boat shot toward the rocks. Salt in my eyes, I didn't see it crash. I sure heard it though—the boat that must've carried hundreds of passengers over the years exploded like a mailbox struck with a baseball bat. Its bits flew into our faces.

I doggy-paddled to the shore and stretched out between the rocks. My backpack was still clutched to my chest. I unzipped it, revealing a thoroughly wet, but unharmed blue ferret. She shook herself out and went to nudge my neck.

"What a ride, huh?" I said weakly.

The dark elves crawled out onto the sand beside me. Coria rolled over to puke into a pile of seaweed.

"So much for that belly of steel," I told her.

Strands of black hair plastered across her face, she grinned at me.

"You're a nutjob, demigod," she rasped. "And thank Abnoba for that."

When my head stopped spinning, I went to retrieve my daggers. Leshi's ball of thread was tied to what was left of the boat, which wasn't much. I unwound it from the wheel and untied Sila. Veter dislodged from the oak and flew into my hand. The clouds that had seemed black and angry just minutes ago, were clearing to reveal the pink-tinged, perfect azure sky. The World Tree was enormous over my head. It was impossible to see the top. I heard a flutter of wings above me, and then stared up at the branches of the oak.

Several pairs of eyes stared down at me. The size of a small woman, they were birds from the neck down. Their feathers were gray, and the tips of their wings were tinged with red that looked like blood. Their human faces were hawkish and sharp-featured as they stared down at me. It was in that moment that I knew without a doubt that they had called the storm to kill us.

"Yeah?" I said. "And how did that work out for you?"

I heard Tynan's heavy footsteps behind me.

"Sirins," he growled. "This isn't good."

"Can you fight?" I asked him quietly.

He grunted in affirmation.

A voice came from everywhere at once.

"Let them pass, my daughters," it echoed in the branches and ricocheted off the rock. Its deep, sensuous timbre sent a shiver down my spine. "They have earned the right."

The sirins lifted into the air, and I got a good look at their wing span. If they looked big enough to carry off a sheep, what did their mother look like?

"Approach, Dmitry Dolyavich," the same deep voice echoed from all around us. "Let us speak."

14

THE ROOTS OF THE World Tree coiled like the feet of a tentacled giant. Up close, I couldn't see around them. We stood at the foot of it like it was a mountain. Once again, I tilted up my head to see if I could find the top. Maybe the whole point was that there wasn't one, and its boughs reached into infinite worlds. Realities upon realities.

Coria looked giddy, and Tynan looked apprehensive as we stepped between the bulbous growths. Alysa was so still around my neck, someone could have mistaken her for an azure scarf. The sirins screeched as they flew into an entry in the root work. I couldn't help but check my shirt. It looked as miserable as my sore, bruised hands. It didn't feel right to talk to a prophetess looking like I'd been run over by a steam roller. On the other hand, if she wanted me to look presentable, maybe she shouldn't have tried to kill us. We followed the rustle of wings into the dark.

The dark didn't last long. Light filtered through the gaps in the roots and checkered the ground. Dust danced in pockets of sunlight. This made the shadows seem impenetrable in contrast. I kept going until my eyes adjusted. Then, I cringed as my sneaker crunched on a bone. I looked down and saw a very human-looking femur sticking out of the ground. Yikes. Coria sniffed behind me, and I heard Tynan slide out his sword. Those two have seen plenty of monster lairs, but even I've watched enough supernatural crime shows to recognize a human-eating one.

"Stay in the backpack," I told Alysa. She slipped through the zipper opening without a sound.

"Dmitry," the same deep, carrying voice came from above me. I looked up and saw a burst of red and a pair of deep-seated eyes. They were bright green and seemed to glow in the gloom. "Welcome. You traveled hard to find the answer you seek."

"Could've traveled a little easier," I said, "if it wasn't for your storm."

A dry laughter came from the dark. "Oh, but we have so very few visitors. My daughters are starved for entertainment."

I looked around and saw dozens of smaller forms clustered in the pockets. Their wings rustled and their eyes bore down on us. Entertainment wasn't the only thing they looked starved for. Better play it safe.

Awkward, I bowed. "Gamayun the prophetess," I said. "Thank you for seeing me."

Green eyes sparked with humor and drew closer. A face emerged into the light, then a body. I was relieved to see that unlike the more awkward Google search results, the Gamayun didn't actually have an—ahem—anatomically-correct torso. The feathers started just below the collar bones. Leave it to the pervs in the Middle Ages to put boobs on a bird.

"That's better," she crooned. "No one likes an impolite boy."

The wings were entirely red and the specks of crimson went up her wings and onto her shoulders. From there, it specked the skin and the gray of her other feathers. Her face was both terrifying and more beautiful than I was comfortable staring at. She was easily seven feet tall from feet to head, and her wing span was double that. Her face looked young, but she must've been very, very old. Definitely had seen the likes of me before. Eaten a few, too.

"Does your grandmother know you're here?" she asked in a tone that implied that she knew she didn't.

"Why is everyone asking me that?" I inquired.

"An unbound demigod, the apple of Yaga's eye?" she chortled and her eyes took on a scary shimmer. Her claws looked very big as she shifted from one leg to another. "I wouldn't wander into too many places alone, young Dmitry."

I squared my shoulders. "I'm not here to talk about family relations."

"Of course," she nodded gravely. "You've come here to ask about your human world. Alas, I cannot see through the veil between pantheons."

My heart sank down my throat. "It has to do with Vyraj."

"Ask your question, and we shall see."

I paused, feeling the roof of my mouth. This felt like an asking-a-genie-for-a-wish-type situation. Where one wrong word could turn you from an immortal fashion model into a mannequin. Choosing my words carefully, I said:

"What is the cause of portals to Vyraj opening in Salt Lake City area, and are they closing in around me?"

Gamayun jumped down to a lower branch to gaze upon us. Her eyes were intense in the semi-darkness. I could see her hair, straight and raven-black, hanging down to obscure her features as she stared down at us.

"Are you sure that is the question that you want to ask?" she asked sweetly.

Numb, I nodded. I wasn't sure. At all. But showing weakness to a bird of prey seemed like a bad idea.

"As you wish." She straightened and her wings shifted down like a pair of crimson red swords. "The cause of the portals are rooted in Vyraj," she said. "For I can see it. A bond that stretches out through the fabric of the world. It is reaching for its missing piece. Vyraj is reaching for its missing piece."

There were only two connections to Vyraj in Utah. And only one in Salt Lake.

"Are you saying," I asked. "That I'm the reason the portals are opening in the city?"

The cave erupted in echoing laughter. All around us, sharp talons gripped the roots of the World Tree as the sirins joined their mother in her mirth.

"Are you?" she asked sweetly. "Not that it matters now."

I planted my feet into the ground, and refused to cower, even as a little voice in my head screeched "Run, you idiot! Run, run, run!"

"What is that supposed to mean?"

The Gamayun smiled sweetly. Her teeth were rows of toothpicks on her otherwise human face.

"It means that your precious Yav city will be safe after today." Her daughters inched closer, and I saw their eyes glow in the dark. "Since there will not be a cause for Vyraj to reach for it." She spread out her wings, all fourteen feet of them. "Yaga is the one who imprisoned me here. And here you are, her truest affection, walking into my home. To ask for *my* wisdom." She laughed and the sound carried. Her daughters picked it up, multiplying it by the dozen until the cave was filled with her cold amusement. "Die, young Dmitry."

15

THE SIRINS BOMBED US. My daggers swept left and right, but they were almost useless in close combat. Sirins were damn fast and their talons could rival kitchen knives. Tynan's sword was more effective. The sirins gave him a wider birth. They kited him like a video game boss, attacking and flying away.

Sick of being out-daggered, I rolled out of the way of raking claws and let Veter fly. It pierced a sirin in the shoulder that had Coria by the hair. Before she saw where I was, I slipped between an opening in the roots. Then, I called Veter back into my right hand. It pulled out of the creature's shoulder with a wet slurp. The sirin wailed and lifted into the air.

As much as I hated leaving Coria and Tynan in the middle of the cave floor, I was much more use off the ground. Veter sang as I pinned the birds to their perches, materializing next to them. My first kill had been easy. As soon as the others clued into the demi who could teleport at will and gut them where they stood, they were faster to lift off. I soon found out that it wasn't just their talons I had to watch out for. Their wings were tipped with thorns, and I received a gash across my ribs that cut too close to some vital giblets. I needed my giblets, damn it. Throwing Veter at an empty nest, I materialized atop. My sneakers crunched over bones as I crouched out of sight to assess the situation.

Tynan had made the smart choice to move himself and Coria against the side of a root. His sword flashed in the dimness as he warded off the sirins from his charge. Feathers flew and blood splattered. Both he and Coria were sporting scrapes and wounds. At first, it looked like the female elf was cowering in her armiger's shadow. Then, I saw her hands tap over her suitcase, as if she was opening a puzzle.

Brutal and efficient, Tynan moved through the incoming threats with practiced precision. I was surprised at the grace with which he handled his ridiculous anime sword. Slashing and thrusting, he picked the sirins out of the air. Two attacked at the same time, and he sliced a talon off one before digging into the wing of another.

He spun and parried. Like a living wall protecting his charge, he moved back and forth at an angle. Coria kept working without looking up. I wondered how many times they'd done this. It took an unimaginable amount of trust on her part to not question that her armiger would protect her.

More birds came at Tynan, and for a moment, I lost sight of the elves. When the winged wall cleared, I saw a sirin get lucky, passing Tynan's defenses. Face full of bloodlust, her talons extended to Coria. I let Veter sing through the cave. It disappeared into the back of the sirin's neck. She dropped to the ground.

The Gamayun screeched overhead.

"Where are you, Dolyavich?" she demanded. "Come and face me!"

I followed Veter down to Coria and landed next to her in a crouch.

"Nice of you to drop in!" she said.

"I was busy—" I slashed Sila at a claw coming at me,"—unlike you!"

Her grin ferocious, Coria thrust her hand *into* her suitcase. "Done!"

"What—"

Her hand emerged from inside the leather, leaving the surface unharmed. A vial glistened in her hand.

"Takes a moment—" she panted, "—to unbind it." She pulled the cork out with her teeth. "Tynan!" she called overhead.

The armiger glanced down, and his eyes widened. He grabbed me by the back of my shirt.

"Get away from her!" he yelled.

Not having a clue what was going on, I let the elf stagger us backwards.

Coria threw me a vicious grin and drank the potion.

A burst of light blinded me. The sirins screeched and fell out of the air. When I finally could see again, Coria was doubled over. Her body twitched and rippled.

"What's happening?" I asked Tynan.

"She's transmuting," he said.

"She's what—"

Coria's form swelled and ripped through her clothes. Her neck snapped and a muzzle grew where her face had been. Her shoulders burst out of her tank top. They rippled with muscle. Where the bird-boned dark elf had been now stood an honest-to-god werewolf. It was at least seven feet tall.

Coria—wolfy?—threw her head back and howled. I grabbed the straps of my backpack, glad that Alysa was safely inside.

"Holy shit!"

The werewolf tore at the stunned sirins. New blood dotted the air. Seeing the threat on the ground double, the sirins rose into the air and circled my companions like vultures. Outraged by the death of their sisters, they came down at Coria with new ferocity. Tynan pushed me aside and ran to his mistress, bloodied sword bare. I started to follow him when a pair of blood-red talons dug into my shoulders.

A laugh came overhead and I saw Gamayun's green eyes flash down at me.

"There you are!" Her freakishly pretty lips opened over teeth that would make Pennywise jealous. "I will make a meal out of you!" she said. Her head lowered to see me more closely and I thrust my daggers up at her ankle. Sila dug deep and she screeched in pain. The injured leg dropped me and I dangled from her grasp. Her wings beat up and we lifted fifteen feet into the air. My left shoulder went numb from her claws and I tried to stab her other talon with Veter, but my position was too awkward to stab upward. My vision blackened around the edges. Even though I couldn't feel it, I suspected I was losing blood.

The back of my head struck hay as Gamayun slammed me down into her nest. Small animal bones crunched under me. I smelled dead rodents and wet feathers. Her talon pressed against my throat and squeezed.

"You and your friends made a mess of this," she hissed. "Why didn't you die like a good boy?"

I choked putrid air into my lungs. "Never...been...good...at...that."

Her talon squeezed. "You killed a lot of my daughters. Now, you'll have to die slowly."

Up close, she looked less like a woman and more like an ancient predator that liked playing with her prey.

Something scrambled under my back, but I was too busy dying to care.

"You... can make more... right?" I rasped.

The Gamayun shrilled and I closed my eyes. Here came my death. Where did demigods go when they died, anyway?

Instead of blackness, I felt her talon lift off my throat. She was still shrilling, the sound high-pitched and desperate. Had I hit my head? I unglued my eyes. Above me, Gamayun tried tearing at her face, but wasn't very effective. That's what happens when you have wings instead of hands.

A blue shape hung from her eyelid. A long, noodely body was clawing at her cheek. Alysa had gotten out of the backpack and was now saving my undeserving bacon. The Gamayun howled. Her wings were beating a small hurricane into the air as she shook her head to dislodge the ferret.

I scrambled back in the nest and felt around for my daggers. Sila and Veter lay where I'd dropped them. The sudden rush of oxygen and adrenaline cleared my head. My eyes found Tynan and Coria. They were bloodied but still standing on their two—four?—feet. The elf's sword was drenched in blood, and he was visibly limping as he and the werewolf circled back to back. Coria's muzzle was covered in blood, and her left claw was limp at her side.

Aiming at a root next to them, I let Veter fly.

"Time to go!" I yelled and grabbed Alysa. The ferret came off the Gamayun with the grossest tearing sound I've ever heard in my life. Blood streamed down the prophet bird's face. My fist around the ferret's soft belly, I zoomed down. Distance from the bird seemed like the best policy.

Sliding off the root, I jumped to Tynan's side. Up close, the elf looked even worse. His dark gray complexion had lightened from exhaustion. Red eyes frantic, he almost took off my head with his spine sword.

"Whoa! Whoa!" I put up my palms. "It's me!"

Coria spun to face me. Her hide was gnarled and stained with blood. It was impossible to tell if it was hers or the sirins'. Strings of tissue and feathers stuck out between her teeth.

They kept coming at us. Feathers, wings and claws, and glowing eyes. I couldn't see the roof of the cavern. I parried and slashed. My back pressed to Coria and Tynan as we did our best to protect each other. As I got knocked down to my knees when the bodies of sirins pressed on us from above, I eyed the ground briefly. If I bled and said the words, maybe we could be saved. My lips opened. Then, they closed. I would be bound forever. I could kiss my brewery goodbye. I could kiss my peace goodbye. Drops of blood blackened the already dark ground. I couldn't do it. I just couldn't. I pushed off the ground and faced the threats as they came—one at a time.

"You will die!" the Gamayun screeched over our heads. Her voice told me that she wasn't playing with her prey anymore. My adrenaline turned to icy panic. "My daughters cover the island, and their talons will tear you apaaaart!"

Alysa screeched on my shoulder and Tynan's red eyes widened with the first show of fear I'd ever seen on his face.

"Come on," I said to him. "We killed a ton of them already. How many more can there be?"

My answer came in a deafening sound of wings. The sunny pockets of light on the ground disappeared as bird bodies piled in from outside. There were so many that they blocked out the sun, preventing any light from seeping through the roots. I looked up as sirins thumped down on perches. There were dozens, no—scores—of them.

"You demand to be a hero?" the Gamayun howled. "Then die a hero's death!"

The three of us pressed our backs against each other. Something crunched underfoot, and I felt the flat surface of Coria's suitcase under my sneaker. I could smell my own sweat. Coria panted to my right and Tynan swore in Feuerzunge to my left. The sentiment was unanimous—we were thoroughly fucked.

Alysa's wet nose nudged my cheek.

"I know," I said to her. "It was fun while it lasted."

She crossed over my right shoulder to my left, then settled at the back of my neck. Her chirping sounded reassuring, and for a moment I didn't understand. Then, it dawned on me.

"No," I said. "Don't do it! It's too early, you will tear yourself to shreds." She chirped again, quieter this time.

The Gamayun flew down. Wings spreading, she hovered in the air above us. Her left eye was a spot of bloodied gore. She wasn't smiling anymore.

"Kill them!" she commanded.

Wings spread and mouths opened in shrieks. I saw talons and crimson feathers.

A screech came from over my head. The bloodied face of Gamayun fell from the sky.

"Die!" she screeched.

The roots around us and the dead bodies of the sirins smudged in my vision, as if someone poured water over paint. Alysa pulled us through realities.

16

WET ASPHALT SPLIT MY knees. Veter and Sila clattered on the pavement. I rolled over until I hit grass. I groaned and doubled over, my bleeding shoulder squirting something thick between my fingers. Looking down, I saw blood staining the lawn under me.

I heard a train and smelled freshly cut grass mixed with gasoline. Factory smoke rose in the distance. I recognized the road that disappeared toward a ghetto. We were in west Salt Lake.

In my peripheral vision, I saw Coria roll on the ground. She was back to her human self and buck-naked. Lifting herself to all fours, her spine curved as she retched. Bright blue liquid slithered between her lips and sloshed on the pavement. She pulled her long dark hair away from her face and sat back on her haunches. Her sleek, athletic body was stark in the moonlight, but that's not what had my attention.

The blue contents of her stomach *slithered*. The mass moved and spread over the asphalt. It swelled until it grew to the size of a small heap. Then, the heap doubled, and tripled. It grew legs and hair.

Rising off the ground, the werewolf, just like the one Coria had turned into in the cave, looked around wildly. Its muzzle pulled back to reveal blood-stained teeth. It looked at Coria, then at Tynan as he popped out of the air next to his mistress. For a moment, I thought it would attack us. Injured as we were, we were definitely easy prey. There was hesitation in the shifting lines of its body. Its nose tilted up at the half-moon in the smoggy sky. With a sniff and a whine, it turned and started toward the railroad. The meaning of what Coria had called herself, a transmute, now made more sense. She had the power to turn herself into creatures that she captured. If only I didn't feel like shredded beef, I would've appreciated the coolness.

I lifted myself off the ground and clasped my roiling stomach. Alysa had saved us—

Alysa!

I fumbled around in the dark until I found her. The sight of the tiny, unmoving body on the ground made my heart drop. I crawled to her. You could barely see the blue fur under the blood.

"Oh..." My hands shook as I stroked her back. I made myself get closer and stroke her muzzle. I didn't dare roll her over. She was so fragile. I drew closer to the ferret and gently scooped her up. Her body was nearly weightless in my palms. At first it felt cold and still. Then, a barely audible whine escaped her. I gently parted the matted fur at her throat, looking for heartbeat. A slow thump pushed at my finger. She was alive.

"Veles eternal," I whispered. "We need to get home."

Luckily, Min-Ho found us before the cops did. The goblin never turned off his phone, which I had always found annoying before. Twenty minutes after I called him, the headlights of my Mazda pierced the night. I had never seen anything so beautiful.

I slid into the passenger seat. Min-Ho was wearing pajamas with anime kittens on them and his hair was ruffled. I must've pulled him out of bed. Since we lived so close, we all had copies of each other's house and car keys in case of an emergency. A precaution he had agreed to years ago.

Coria was wearing Tynan's shirt that went down to her knees. Tynan, bare-chested and bloodied, helped her climb into the back seat. The guitarist didn't ask who they were, but I felt him scan their supernatural signatures as his magic tingled my skin. His eyes went to Alysa on my lap.

"What happened?" he asked.

I told him the gist of it. Not feeling like going into the details, I was grateful when he didn't push. I rubbed the shifter's tiny head. Guilt was pounding like a headache in my temples. I should've gone to Baba Yaga for help. My pride, as Leshi predicted, had put everyone at risk. And now Alysa—

"Can you save her?" I asked the goblin.

He didn't answer as he took the exit to our house.

"James is at his parents' for the weekend," he said finally. "I will stay the night and see what I can do."

We piled out of the car in the light of the street lamps. My garden's fairy lights didn't fill me with the same joy they usually did. I carried Alysa's limp form over the threshold of the house. It was good that my roommate was out. I was in no mood to explain the thrilling world of the supernatural to him today.

"Master, who are these strangers?" Domo asked when he saw the grim-faced Coria and Tynan step into the living room. Then, he addressed my obvious torn apart look. "And what happened to your clothes? I had just washed them." At least he had his priorities straight.

I didn't reply to the house spirit and walked past him into the kitchen. In my hands, Alysa was drawing short, ragged breaths. I swept the leftover Chinese food off the table and placed her down.

"What's happening to her?" I asked the goblin as he braced his hands over her.

"Her portal power is strained. Her magic is unweaving itself."

I swallowed. "What does that mean?"

He held my eyes. "She *is* magic. It means that the threads holding her together are coming undone." His gentle fingers rolled her over. Pulling down the neckline of his shirt, he untangled an amulet from his collection of charms. "My mother's healing charm." He pulled it over his head. He placed the charm on Alysa's matted fur. "I will also draw her a bujeok." At my uncomprehending stare, he explained. "A healing talisman. But it will take some time. I'll draw you one, too." He nodded at my wound, that I'd all but forgotten about. His eyes looked at me with pity, which made me feel like an even bigger piece of shit than I already was. "Go take a shower. You stink."

I checked on Coria and Tynan. The two of them sat in the middle of the living room. Their sword and suitcase lay between them. They quietly conversed in Feuerzunge and looked up when I came in.

"Thank you," I said to them. "Truly. We wouldn't have made it out alive if it wasn't for you two."

Coria perked up. "Will she live then?"

My lips pressed together as unshed tears burned on my eyeballs. "I don't know," I said.

She nodded, and stood up to place a hand on my shoulder. Tynan's face didn't hold the usual distaste when he looked at me, which made me feel even worse.

"You fought bravely," she said. "Did you get the answer you sought?"

Oh, did I ever. Not only did I possibly kill my friend, I was the reason the portals were opening all over my city. It had been my fault from the beginning.

"I need a shower," I said and gently released myself from her hold. "Domo!"

I asked the domovoi to give the elves blankets and show them the guest bathroom. Seeing that I wasn't in the mood for shenanigans, the spirit obeyed with unusual promptness. Afterward, I went down to my basement.

There, I stripped off my stinking jeans and blood-caked shirt. Standing in my underwear, I looked over my injuries with little interest. My ribs were scarred and caked with blood and there were puncture wounds on my shoulder from where the Gamayun had snatched me into the air. They ached at my touch, which told me the punctures were infected. I pressed the heels of my palms to my eyes. What was I thinking? I told myself Min-Ho could save her. But who could be sure? I blamed myself for every scratch on her tiny body. If only I'd had the balls to claim my mother's power back in the cave. Tynan had been right. I was a coward. For the first time in years, I felt the weight of my choices.

I washed my battered body. I found clean clothes and put on the pants but didn't bother to put on the shirt. I made my way upstairs. Min-Ho sat in the same place I left him, drawing on a square of yellow paper with red ink.

"This is a healing bujeok," he said at my questioning glance. "She's still breathing. It should help." He looked over my torn torso. "Here." Holding out his hand, his pushed another yellow square toward me. "This one's for you."

Not sure what else to do, I pressed it to my shoulder, and felt the pain ebb. I reached into my first aid kit and found a bandage strip. Doing my best with one hand rolling and one hand holding it down, I wrapped my torso.

Domo popped up in front of me. "Here, master." He held a tube of anti-bacterial gel in his hand. "Allow me."

I let him apply the salve and wrap my shoulder. My body felt better. Not that I cared. My eyes were glued to the table where my friend of the last four years drew in shallow, bloody breaths.

"I'm going to the gas station," I said. "We'll need painkillers."

Min-Ho nodded without looking up from his work.

Not wanting to face the elves, I slipped out the back. In the dark, I breathed the scent of wet grass and ripening apples. My garden, as perfect as it's always been, twinkled with fairy lights that I'd strung up last summer. The arches creaked from the weight of the grapes and the neat rows of herbs and vegetables perfumed the air. My little kingdom, that I fought to preserve at all costs. Too high of a cost. I wanted to punch something. The only thing I had done with my hesitation was hurt the ones I cared about. For years, I'd sat in my garden like a fat slug. I walked down the street. Pain killers were only an excuse. I needed to think.

Hands in pockets, I headed toward the nearest 24-hour gas station. The night was punctuated by loud music spilling out of cars and girls laughing in the passenger seats. A few days ago, I would've thrown a party while James was out, just to piss him off. Somehow, I was no longer in a partying mood.

The sound of a sizzle came from my right, and I saw a portal split open in mid-air. Gods damn it. Nothing came out of it, but it was only a matter of time. I jogged to it, and used my needles to sew it shut. It shimmered and disappeared into the fabric of the universe. The only thing I could do now was hope to Veles that Alysa survived. Then, I had to chase the monsters out of Salt Lake. I was sure Coria would be thrilled at the opportunity to capture a few stragglers. What came after that, I had no idea. Somehow, I needed to figure out how to keep the portals from opening. If they were really opening because of me, I had to find a way.

I took a shortcut past a bank to get to the gas station. The smell of smoke stopped me in my tracks.

"What the hell," I murmured.

I followed the smell and it took me to the drive-thru with the ATM. The trees studding the dark lawn didn't sway in the wind I could feel in my hair. Anxiety nipped at my innards. Something was wrong. Very wrong.

I curled my fingers around the knitting needles at my waist.

Bam!

A blast of hot air had me staggering backwards and bits of brick lacerated my cheeks. The one-story bank went up in flames. I watched the fire burst through the windows and start spreading across the lawn. My hair seemed to sizzle in the sudden heat. I watched the fire, slack-jawed. Alarms blared. Hopefully no one was working late into the night.

I slapped my pockets. My phone was at home. I started across the lawn to where I thought the blast had come from—around the other side of the building. Maybe there was a short and something exploded. Maybe the clerks ran a meth lab in the basement. There wouldn't be any point trying to put out the inferno, but maybe the firefighters could contain the flames to keep them from spreading out to the neighborhood houses. Smoke struck my nose as the heat rolled off the building.

Something jumped out of the fire. Against the flames, it was a dark silhouette. I couldn't see the details, but it was unmistakably *feline*. Then it drew closer and my cheeks went numb.

A giant black cat the size of a rottweiler stared at me with flaming eyes. Fire burst from the tip of its long tail. It was an ovinnik. I hadn't seen one in years, but there was no mistaking it.

"Oh," I breathed. "Shit."

The ovinnik meowed. A blaze started at its feet and set the nearest bush on fire.

"It's funny how things can go wrong so quickly," a raspy voice said behind me in Old Slav. "Isn't it, cousin?"

17

S LOWLY, I TURNED TOWARD the voice. I *really*, really didn't want to.

"Something could sit there for years," the voice continued. "Then poof! An old generator topples over and exposes a wire. A leak finds a spark." The man's cackle turned into a racking cough. "You know what I'm talking about?"

The man standing behind me looked about thirty. His raspberry-colored jacket and Adidas pants made him look like a young gopnik from a Russian hood. His hair was cropped to a buzz like a cancer patient's. He resembled a broken old whip. Sinewy, damaged, but still dangerous. Eyes seated deep in dark circles, he looked as I remembered him—three weeks short on sleep. It was his smile that made me almost whiz my pants. He smiled at me like a rat smiles at a fat cockroach.

"Golo," I whispered.

The demigod of bad luck winked at me. His teeth gleamed in the light of the fire. "Hi, Dmitry." Arms spreading out, he stepped toward me. I smothered the urge to bolt. "Aren't you going to give your long-lost cousin a hug?"

He cackled at the stony expression on my face. Reaching behind his ear, he produced a cigarette. The lighter flicked in his hand and he took a long pull. The ember flashed in the small pupils of his eyes.

"How did you find me?" I asked.

He gave me flat look and took another drag of his cigarette. "How do you think?"

My back was covered in sweat and the needles felt slippery in my grasp. "The drekavac," I guessed.

The ovinnik circled around his feet, acting so much like a regular house cat that it gave me the creeps. Every padded step scorched the ground.

"I've been waiting for you to make a mistake for years," Golo said. "But I'm a patient guy. Sometimes, I get lucky, too."

"What do you want?" I asked.

He scoffed. "Don't play stupid, cousin. I want the same thing I wanted twenty years ago." His eyes fell hungrily on my hands that clutched my needles. "Give me Dolya's needles like a good boy. Otherwise, I'll tear out your guts and knit myself a sweater." His cigarette went out. "*Blyat!*" Snapping his lighter, he tried to re-light it. It sparked and smoked. He rolled the wheel furiously with no result.

Watching him struggling with the lighter lifted my spirits a bit. At least, it was still true that Golo suffered as much bad luck as he dealt. Feeling suicidal, I pointed at the flaming bank.

"I think you left a little fire over there," I said.

Golo tossed the lighter and the cigarette into the rising flames. He was no longer smiling.

"Give me the needles, nice and easy," he said. "You can still walk away from this."

I widened my stance. My eyes flicked at another ovinnik that stepped out of the fire and crossed toward us. Those same flamey bastards burned down my tree house. Were they involved in all the pyro shit Golo had been up to for the past hundred years? Undoubtedly.

"Or what?" I asked.

Golo gave me a once-over and hollered.

"Whoo! Baby demi got brave." He stroked the head of a passing fire cat. "Remember the last time you got brave? I do."

"That was a long time ago," I said.

"Was it?" he asked. "To me, it was a blink of an eye." His eyes narrowed as he scanned me. "Still too chicken to take on your mother's mantle, I see. Makes sense. If you do, my siblings will roast you alive."

The fire flared up higher and I felt the side of my face baking.

"Why, Golo?" I asked. "Why do you want them? You can't even use them."

He shrugged. "Memento."

I wasn't buying it. "You want them for something," I guessed. When I was a child, it had seemed as if he had been torturing me for nothing. Tying me to trees in the middle of the winter, setting my sanctuary on fire. Regular beatings. All those things seemed like a whim. Now, seeing his face twitch, I thought different. "What is it?"

"It's none of your business," he said. I saw a flash of irritation on his face. "There are bigger things at play." He hunched his shoulders and stuffed his hands in his pockets. "What you should be concerned about are the consequences of your choices here. I know about your house and your bar. The one nearby here? They would look great—" he snapped his fingers as if looking for the right word, "in flames."

Hair prickled at the back of my neck. He grinned at my expression.

"Did you think you could hide them forever?" He laughed. "Very optimistic. And stupid."

Panic pushing up my throat, I played the only card I had. "You wouldn't dare. Grandmother—"

"Has no power in Yav," Golo finished for me. "When she sent you here, she left you on your own. Time to stop hiding behind her skirts and smell the fire." He scratched behind his ear. "I don't have to be a dick about this. I don't care about your little house, or your little life. You're not even at the top of my kill list."

"Right," I murmured. "That's why you've been stalking me."

He ignored me. "I'll give you until tomorrow night," he said.

"What if I run?" I said.

"From all you've built?" He snorted. "I know you better than that." We both knew that he was right and he smiled in satisfaction. "It's for the best, anyway. What the hell do you need those needles for? They're nothing but a target on your back. You wanna get rid of me once and for all? Here is your golden opportunity." He grimaced and spat on the ground. "I know what you're thinking. How are you going to close these portals if you don't have your needles?"

"How did you—"

"I know everything the monsters know, remember?" he said. "Don't worry about them. Once you give me the needles, Vyraj won't be your problem anymore. You're the reason they're opening, aren't you?" He read the answer on my face. "You can relax. After years of clenching your butthole at every noise in your backyard, wouldn't that be nice?" He cackled.

The sound of sirens came whining from a distance. Someone must've seen the fire and called 911.

He made a low whistling noise. One by one, four more shapes leapt out of the flaming bank. Ovinniks' meows filled the air as they circled my cousin like a howling choir.

"Think about it," he said. "There is only one of you, and there are five of us. And I'm the *nice* one. Renounce the needles. Your mother's legacy will be your death. Be smart, little cousin." His sunken eye winked at me. "See you tomorrow night."

His form began to smoke. The ovinniks leapt toward him and their joint fire made a conflagration that consumed Golo's body. He went up like a torch. In seconds, they were gone. What was left behind was a plume of smoke, the sirens, and me who looked very much like an arsonist about to be caught at the scene of the crime.

My legs wooden, I made it out of there. I thought I could still smell Golo's cigarette smoke and hear his raspy laughter.

18

THE GRAYING SKY PROMISED dawn by the time I got home. Coria was asleep on the couch. Tynan slept sitting up on the floor, his back against the cushions at her feet. He woke the second I stepped into the living room. I waved at him and he nodded. Domo was nowhere to be seen.

In the kitchen, I checked on Alysa. She was wrapped in a fluffy kitchen towel and was covered in bujeoks that hung off her like little yellow flags. Min-Ho must've gone to sleep in the spare bedroom. I dimmed the kitchen light and checked her injuries. Her belly looked less raw. It rose and fell regularly, and I thought her breathing sounded clearer. Maybe that was just my wishful thinking.

I pulled up a stool and sat next to her. Someone had brought a bottle of white from my basement. I picked up the bottle and fingered the peeling label. It pictured a smiling woman wearing a grapevine wreath on her strawberry-blond hair. James had helped me design the label last year. I had been so proud of it. This was going to lead my first line of wines. I wanted to hurl it against the wall.

My cousin had finally found me. If I was honest with myself, I wasn't that surprised. As he had said, it was going to happen eventually. I set the knitting needles in front of me on the table. They glinted dully. This was my mother's legacy. Fire and killer birds and wrestling bears. My grandmother, too, and the pink sky of Vyraj. The needles were the last thing that tied me to that world. And Golo would burn my home for them.

The footsteps behind me were so soft, I almost missed them. I looked up to see Tynan. The elf took the chair opposite me and sat, his sword on his lap. He looked as out of place in my kitchen as I felt.

"I'll help you hold vigil," he said. "Where were you?"

"My cousin found me," I told him. I'm not sure why I bothered, but the words came rolling off my tongue. "He wants the needles. He'll be there tomorrow night to take them."

Tynan humphed.

"I know what you're thinking," I said bitterly.

He raised a perfect eyebrow. "You do?"

"Same thing you thought from the beginning." My lip curled. "That I'm a coward." I took a deep breath. "You're right."

"I don't think you're a coward," the elf said. "Coria chastised me in Vyraj and she was right. I was wrong about you. I think you were brave on that island and you saved our lives."

I glanced up at him, surprised. "Did you hit your head when we portalled back or something?"

He laughed a deep, melodic laughter. "You think you're the only who has ever struggled with loyalty? Wondered where you belong?"

"You never have," I said.

Shaking his head, he steepled his fingers. "I too have struggled with facing responsibility."

I snorted. "Yeah, right. What did you do, slice a manticore's head off *too* hard in honor of your tribe?" Leaning back in my chair, I threw my hands behind my neck and eyed him with scorn. "I haven't visited my grandmother in twelve years. *Twelve*. I've had every opportunity and I blew them all off."

"You had your reasons," he said.

"You don't know what I did. My cousins are tearing the world apart, and I hide here like a cowar—" I started.

"I sent Coria off to die."

That cut me short.

Tynan took a deep breath, and his red eyes dropped down. His long fingers drummed on the table.

"When I was younger," he started, "I was assigned to guard Coria on her first monster runs. She was..." He gave a rueful laugh. "You know. *Coria*. Fierce and proud and smart. Beautiful. For three years we were inseparable. I had feelings for her. Abnoba's mercy. I was *mad* for her."

I crossed my arms over my chest and looked at him in bewilderment. I had never expected him to open up to me.

"At first, I couldn't dare to hope. Then, I became resentful. I wanted her to abandon tradition and marry me, instead. Her mothers' wishes be damned."

"But she's not attracted to men," I said.

"I wanted her to make an exception." He smiled ruefully. "To see me as more than an armiger."

I had to admit that if a girl could go straight for anyone, it would be the pretty-as-a-picture Tynan.

Intrigued, I found a glass and poured him a serving of the white wine. The delicate aroma of apricots lifted into the air. I had a feeling he wasn't comfortable opening up. Before now, I don't think I'd heard him say more than two sentences to me. Not that I had any idea what had changed, but I did the thing I was best at. I poured him a drink like a seasoned bartender—right on cue. He took the glass gratefully.

"And then what happened?"

"Coria is a transmute," he said. I nodded, indicating that I knew. "Her family line traps monsters and uses their *gutus solis*. Her responsibilities are greater than mine. That year, while I was pining after her like some lonesome pup, she was preparing to face Zugut in battle."

I frowned, remembering. "The rival tribe."

He grunted in agreement and took a sip of the wine. "They've been after our land for centuries." His eyes widened, and he stared at the glass, then at me. "This is exceptional, demigod."

"I know," I said and smothered the flare of pride. Now was not the time to feel proud of myself. "Please continue."

"On the eve of the battle, we quarreled. This was going to be her first real trial and I feared for her survival. I pressed her to stay home and run away with me while her mothers headed their army. She refused. She called me—what's the word you're so fond of?—a coward." He gave me a rueful smile. "That shattered my fragile pride. I stormed off, leaving her to face the morning alone." His fingers traced the rim of the glass. "I fled to the Black Stretch, the desert hills where the volcanoes had burned and died thousands of years ago, leaving an uninhabitable wasteland. My heart was broken forever, or so I thought. A void so deep no one could bridge it again!" He chuckled into his drink. "Oh, the dramatic folly of my youth."

"But you went back?" I pressed him.

He nodded thoughtfully. "I did. After two days of starving myself in my devastation, I realized that there was one thing that was worse than not being Coria's lover."

"What was that?" I asked.

"Failing her," he said simply. "My heart pulled me back. There was a space that could only be filled by protecting her and making my tribe proud. I couldn't stay away. When I rushed back and found her in the battle field, I felt whole again. Have you ever felt like that?"

I bit my cheek. I *had* felt like that. That day in Vyraj, I had felt whole. Like a missing puzzle piece I had lost under the couch had finally slid into place.

"I'm guessing you saved her," I said.

"That I did, demigod," he agreed. "She had been the last transmute standing in her troop. Even if I didn't win her love in the way I wanted, I was her armiger and the pride of my people." He finished his glass. "A man can be more than one thing. He can love more than one thing. And he can fight for both. For all my folly, I made it back in time and saved her life."

"Better late than never," I murmured.

Tynan stood up and slid his sword into the scabbard over his shoulder. The pommel dinged the kitchen chandelier and it swung, precariously, over our heads.

"I was hard on you when we met because you reminded me of my younger self." He crossed his arms over his chest. "My candor doesn't mean that I don't think you're a fool who indulges in idle things. I just didn't want you to think that you're more special than you already do," he said. His red eyes twinkled. "Just to clarify my intentions."

I smiled. "Hearing you loud and clear."

He nodded.

After he left, I stroked Alysa's fur and looked at the clock. It was six in the morning. I was worn out to the bone. When was the last time I had actually slept?

My needles were warm under my touch as I lifted them off the table. The only thing my mother left me. I remembered the pride I felt when they turned into daggers for the first time. They had never failed me since. Sila and Veter swelled in my hands. I felt the heft of them. How could I fail them now?

Somehow, in a way that escaped me, I was responsible for the portals. And Golo. And my home. I tilted the daggers so they gleamed in the kitchen light. My responsibility. No one else's.

I made myself think. Golo had been too forthcoming about his plans. Too *nice*, in his own words. Why not burn my house down first, and *then* demand the needles, when my spirit was already crushed? He gave me a choice. Give up the needles and live a safe, human life. Even if a large part of me was tempted, something smelled rotten.

"Screw that," I said out loud. "Screw safe."

My head spun, whether it was from the exhaustion or from a realization that suddenly struck me. Now that I had decided there was no way in hell I would go quietly into the night, something became very clear to me. Golo had no intention of leaving my home alone. Why would an arsonist who was responsible for the Burning of Smyrna, and countless villages in Eastern Europe, just walk away from the fun? And why, for that matter, go after something as small and unsatisfying as a house, no matter who it belonged to? There was only one logical conclusion and I didn't like it one bit.

Voices came from the living room. Coria must've woken up. I pushed away from the table and stood up. Walking into the living room, I saw the elves look up at me expectantly.

"Dmitry?" Coria's voice was raspy from sleeping. "What's wrong?"

"I have some good news and some bad news," I announced.

She frowned, and Tynan smiled a secret smile.

"The bad news is that my cousin Golo is here in the city, and he's planning to burn down Salt Lake," I said. Coria opened her mouth to say something, and I lifted a palm into the air to stop her. "The good news is that I know exactly how we can stop him. Will you help me?"

The elf straightened under her blanket. Her crimson eyes lit with avarice. "Will there be monsters?" she asked.

"Veles eternal..." That was one hell of an understatement. Unable to help myself, I laughed. "Yes. Oh, *yes*."

19

Before I did anything else, I took a nice, long nap. Noon greeted me deep in my basement when I heard Domo shuffling about, looking for dirty laundry. I woke up groggy, and with a body that had more aches than not. Fortunately, it was no longer the pain of internal bleeding and the infection that Gamayun had pushed into my shoulder along with her nails. I shuddered when I imagined how much bacteria she carried on those rat-tearing talons. Peeling off the sweat-stained bujeok, I saw that the red markings were gone from the surface. Its magic must've seeped into me while I slept. I could've kissed the goblin.

Upstairs, Min-Ho had lunch waiting. Bagels and hot coffee. Suddenly, I was ravenous.

"I think I'll have to marry you," I told the dokaebbi as I smeared cream cheese on the bagel and topped it with salmon.

His eyebrows lifted. "You couldn't afford my bride-price."

Coria wore James' Dragon Ball Z t-shirt and a pair of shorts I didn't recognize. Domo must not have found anything in James' and my things that could fit Tynan. He sat bare-chested at the table, making the rest of us look like scrawny, underdeveloped teenagers.

"Where's Alysa?" I asked them.

Min-Ho nodded toward the living room. "I carried her to the couch pillows. It looked more comfortable."

"So," Coria's angular face tilted up at me. "You're finally going after your cousin."

I scratched the back of my head. "Technically, he came after me first. But yeah, I know how we can find him."

Now, that I had slept and was thinking more clearly, the gravity of the situation dawned on me. Going after my cousin felt a little like suicide. I decided I no longer cared.

"Golo is crazy dangerous," I told her. "The only thing we have on our side is the element of surprise."

Digging through the kitchen island drawer, I pulled out the map that Alysa and I used to track down Slavic monsters.

"We can't actually see him on this," I explained. "But we can guess where his ovinniks would be. Modern cities don't burn down easily. He'll be focusing on places with wooden structures and a lot of combustibles." I stabbed a finger on the city library. "Example."

The three of them peered at the map. Green dots clustered around the block of downtown.

"They won't start until nightfall," I said.

Coria frowned. "How can you be sure?"

I shrugged. "Golo likes the flames. They're more visible at night. Plus, the human fire trucks are unlikely to respond as quickly as during the day."

Min-Ho shook his head. "We can't know that it's his creatures. The map provides no details. Salt Lake is mostly concrete."

"Tell that to all the nice, historical buildings downtown," I said. "His fire cats can sneak in anywhere. If it's burnable, they will burn it. Inside out, if necessary."

The dokaebbi grunted.

"Fire cats, you say." Coria ran her fingers through her hair. I swear that the ends of her pointy ears trembled in anticipation. "Those would be good for our collection."

"By following Golo to Yav, they've trespassed here. They're fair game. Do you have an—" I searched for the right word, "—essence that could help against them?"

The elves exchange a look. Coria nodded. "I have a frost giant that we caught in Norway last year. But he's a little conspicuous."

"Golo is not exactly subtle either," I said.

"This is Utah," Min-Ho added. "No one believes in creatures here. Whatever supernatural activity anyone sees will be written off as drugs."

I nodded in agreement. "Our goal is to make it through the night," I said. "We can deal with the rest later."

Tynan thrust his chin out. "And Golo himself?"

I smiled. That was the simplest part of my plan, and the most likely to get me killed. Oh, well. "I'll find him myself. Tonight, he's expecting me to cave and give him the needles like a good boy. He thinks he knows me. I'd like to surprise him."

Coria grinned and slapped her palm on the table. "About time."

I watched them discuss strategy over the kitchen table. Their excitement and confidence in their powers made me feel a tingle of hope. No matter how I sliced it, they knew what they were doing. Unlike me. Inside my pocket, I found Leshi's ball of thread. It wouldn't work on humans, but Golo was a creature of Vyraj. In theory, it would find him. As sure as I had sounded with the others, I had no idea how tonight was going to go. It was possible I wouldn't come back. Golo was a fully-fledged demigod. Trying to ambush him with my half-ass powers was a stupid plan, no matter how good I made it sound to my companions.

I heard a rustle and a mumble coming from the living room. My head snapped toward it and I bolted upright. Pushing past Min-Ho, I crossed the carpet to the couch.

Her blue hair strewn across the pillow, Alysa moaned. She was wearing the same shorts she wore to the reservoir and her hair was tangled. Her utterly beautiful human cheeks were flushed with fever, but her breath was even.

My heart lifted and I felt my knees buckle. I sank to my knees in front of the couch. She was alive. She was okay. And she was human again.

I leaned over her and pulled a blanket over her vulnerable-looking shoulders.

"Thank Veles," I murmured.

Her lips moved in her sleep. I could've cried.

Coria came to stand next to me.

"Oh..." The elf leaned closer. "She's... Wow."

"Yep," I said. "She is."

She nudged my shoulder with a grin. "I'll have to introduce myself when she's awake."

"She's not—" I started. "Actually, I don't know." Despite us getting out of a few tough spots together over the years, I didn't know much about her personal life. I had thought that I should keep my one connection to Vyraj at arm's length. What a fool I was.

"It's my problem now," I whispered to Alysa as I tucked a lock of hair behind her ear. "It's always been my problem. I should've listened to you from the start, I'm sorry." She made a little ferrety noise, and I smiled. "I'll finish this."

With a soft pop, Domo materialized next to me. He held a cold compress in his hand.

"I'll take care of her, master," he said gravely.

I glanced at him in surprise. "You will? What happened to 'the enemy' smack talk?"

He looked at me with wide yellow eyes, as if shocked by the question. "She brought you home safe, master! She's an honorable guest." He placed the compress on her forehead. "The goblin did a fine job healing her. Human fever medicine should do the trick from here."

"Thank you, Domo," I said.

His reedy beard twitched in anger. "If master Golo shows up here, I will ward him off. He will burn our home over my cold, dead body!"

I chuckled. "Have you been watching Bruce Willis movies again?" I asked.

In truth, it made me feel much better that Domo was there. His wards wouldn't hold forever against someone as strong as my cousin, but they would last longer than any defense I cooked up.

Tynan and Coria were waiting for me when I rose to my feet.

I gave them as cocky a grin as I could muster.

"You all ready to put out some fires?"

20

D OWNTOWN SALT LAKE GREETED us with the bustling Saturday crowd. The four of us made a plan to meet in the city mall. Coria and I stood waiting on the glass-walled bridge that overlooked the city. The sun was nearing the horizon and the sweaty dusk was cooling to a manageable temperature. From our observation point, we could see the dramatic Gothic peaks of the LDS temple. This time of year, the sun took its sweet time and set after nine. Which meant we had the whole day to prepare for battle.

My new fire retardant jacket hung off my elbow. Min-Ho had bandaged a bujeok for resilience and strength on my bicep and calf. My needles got a knife sheath that hung off my belt. I left my old sneakers on. If push came to shove, a quick getaway was more important than steel-toed boots. Short of shooting my cousin with a bazooka, this was all I could do to up my chances. Everything else was luck. If I could distract Golo long enough, my team could round up the ovinniks and save the city.

"You should let us come with you," Coria said for the hundredth time. She leaned against the glass in her new leather vest that left her tattooed arms bare. Her shimmery fire retardant pants were tucked into combat boots that made her legs look a mile long. Her suitcase was strapped to her back. She looked like a demon bounty hunter from a 90's flick. Even with her illusion spell up, she drew plenty of stares. "I could shift into the giant and make quick work of him."

I shook my head. "Golo is a god-powered badass. You'd waste your giant on him. Besides, I'm just one guy." I shrugged. "If you can keep the city from burning down, you'd save thousands of lives."

Her forehead creased. "As you wish."

I checked the time on my phone and surveyed the crowd. "Where the hell are they?"

As if hearing my frustration, the crowd parted and let through Tynan and Min-Ho.

The elf wore a glistening, silk-fine mail over his torso. His left arm carried a half shield in the shape of a moon. Dark hair pulled up in a pony tail, he looked like something straight out of a video game. Beside him, Min-Ho was grinning a manic grin at my reaction.

"Did you rob Spirit Halloween?" I asked incredulously.

The goblin looked offended. He rattled his knuckles on Tynan's shield. "How dare you? This is pure dwarven moonstone."

I pressed a palm to my forehead. "Where did you even get it?"

"The dwarfs owed me a favor," he said. "This is a loaner."

"What dwarfs?" I demanded. "There are no dwarfs in Salt Lake."

"Old goblin gold makes plenty of friends," he said, as if that explained a damn thing. In fact, it raised more questions than answers, so I decided to stuff it until later to save time.

"What about you?" I asked him.

He grinned an impish grin. Something blurred at his side and I saw his magic part like a magician's cape. At his hip, the green-gemmed hilt of a fighting staff caught rays of sunlight. I recognized the weapon that had given me many bruises in the past.

"I'm good," he said smugly.

"Right," I said. Looking over the three of them, I felt like cannon fodder. "Let's do this."

We clustered toward the end of the bridge, and let the crowd drift past us.

"The wind is moving southwest today," I said. "If I wanted to burn the city, I would start at the Capitol building." I thrust a thumb up at the mountain where the rounded white dome sat among the trees. "Houses up there are hundreds of years old."

I took the map out of my jacket's inner pocket. True to my prediction, a cluster of green dots gathered around the Capitol.

"Then, the library," Coria continued. She glanced up at the goblin. "We should split up."

Min-Ho nodded. "I can take the library."

"The Capitol building is mine," Tynan growled. "If they're planning to move the fire downhill, I can stop them."

Coria took the museum near the temple. The three of them looked at me expectantly. I stared at the map, and shook my head.

"Golo could be anywhere," I said. "I'll separate and go after him." Pulling the ball of thread out of my pocket, I looked at the shimmering fibers. "This is a Vyraj fight."

Pursing her lips, Coria shook her head. Tynan simply nodded and squeezed my shoulder. I thrust the map out to Min-Ho.

"Hold on to this," I said. "I'll need it when I get back."

The goblin looked a little greenish, but took the map.

"Happy hunting," I told the elves.

They saluted me and slid into the crowd.

Before following them, Min-Ho gave me a brief, strong hug.

"Don't get killed, ok?" he said.

"If I do, you'll have to move in with James," I said. "He can't pay rent by himself."

"My point exactly," the goblin said. "The guy is a slob."

I thumped his shoulder, and after a few manly grunts hiding uncomfortable touchy-feelies, he ran after the elves.

Watching him disappear, I tried not to feel utterly alone. Hell, I told myself, I did my best work alone. I fished the ball of thread from my pocket and looked at the fibers. Their multi-hued, liquid glow was strangely comforting. This was going to work. It had to.

I took the escalator down and walked toward the center of the city. There, I slipped between the buildings and hugged the wall until I found a decently deserted alley.

Holding the ball of thread in front of my face, I said in Old Slav:

"Find Golo."

I dropped it. The ball landed on the asphalt. At first it was still, then it shook, as if in indecision.

"Come on," I begged. "Do the thing."

Last thing I needed was for my gamble to fail. If that happened, the only place I would find Golo tonight would be in the ashes of my home. I needed to get to him before he got to Sugar House.

"Golo," I repeated. "The demigod of bad luck. Likho's son."

The thread shimmered and the ball of thread rolled forward down the alley. Pulling on my fire retardant jacket, I followed the path between the buildings and toward the setting sun.

21

THE BALL OF THREAD took me uphill, up the roads to the University of Utah. Just visible enough to be sparkling under the feet of passing students, but not so obvious to be noticed, the clever guide rolled uphill with the confidence of a GPS. I kept my head down, grateful I looked right at home with the partying crowd. No one paid me any attention. I walked unnoticed among the frat boys and the snooty Arts majors to where the shred of Vyraj magic was leading me.

Passing Pizza Pie Pizzeria, I was beginning to wonder if the ball of thread was lost. This wasn't its domain, after all. The sun had set and we'd been walking for nearly an hour. The electro beat from the party houses on the university hill began to roll out of the windows.

We started drawing away from the student housing and toward the campuses themselves. I had to admit that if Golo was nearby, it made sense. Textbooks and desks were excellent fuel. The elaborate campus buildings would undoubtedly survive the fire, but everything inside would be burned.

My head snapped up to the century-old sycamores that lined the campus walkways. Those would go up like torches.

The smell of smoke stopped me in my tracks. I ducked around the corner and only proceeded when it looked clear. Hugging the wall, I stuck to the shadows and away from the street lamps. The ball dimmed and I snatched it up. No sooner than I put it in my coat pocket, the stench of plastic burning hit me full in the face.

An ovinnik stepped around the corner. It wasn't fully aflame, and just looked like a freakishly large cat. I froze in place until it passed. My feet gliding over the grass, I followed it.

"Here kitty, kitty," a voice said in old Slav. It sounded like the guy had smoked a pack a day since he was fourteen and I recognized it immediately. "This is the way in. Squeeze in, you fuzzy moron."

My cousin and three ovinniks stood in front of an AC vent. He was unscrewing a bolt and sliding the panel back. It didn't look big enough to let in one of the giant cats. But then, if normal cats were liquid, that was doubly true of the ovinniks. I looked up at the name of the building and swallowed.

COMPUTER SCIENCE.

Shit.

I fell back, my heart slamming against my ribs. Golo could burn down a building by shorting one computer tower. What about a whole university wing full of them?

Closing my eyes, I counted to five. I could do this. I could catch Golo by surprise and lead him away from the building. For the first time in my life, I wondered how my mother had faced down Likho's creatures. I wished I could ask her.

When I opened my eyes, I saw that I wasn't alone. A pair of feline eyes looked up at me. Fire rolled from the eye sockets and its tail twitched in distaste. An ovinnik. He must've had a pair patrol the area.

The creature hissed, smoke billowing out of its mouth. Its paws left scorch marks on the ground as it paced back and forth.

"What is it?" Golo asked as I did my best to melt into the wall. "Intruders?"

I couldn't let the damn cat demon ruin my element of surprise. Making a split second decision, I threw Veter at a balcony above me. It pierced the window frame of the window behind it. I followed my dagger with Sila. In seconds, I leapt off the grass and my feet landed on the balcony floor. I fell into a crouch.

Footsteps sounded under the balcony.

"There's no one here," Golo said.

The horrible cat gave him a screeching howl.

I let out my breath when he walked away. Eying the rooftop ledge, a very stupid idea came over me.

Veter between my teeth, I climbed higher up. I crawled, the fabric of my jacket snagging on the shingles. When I heard Golo's voice again, it came from directly below me.

"Here we go." Golo said. He lifted something that screeched and I heard a clanking of something like bolts on the pavement. He must've unscrewed another vent.

"A loose bolt, and a spark." My cousin chuckled like a creepy little boy dissecting a frog. His raspberry-colored jacket looked like the color of blood. "When the firefighters finally get through the rubble, the source of the fire will be an accident. Bad, bad luck."

I looked down and saw him open a panel on the wall, and an ovinnik crawled up toward it. Its body changed from a cat to a black slithering mass. Yuck. The tips of its—tail?—ignited and Golo circled his finger around it.

"Get in there," he said. "Start in the middle."

Veter sang through the air and slammed into the vent next to the ovinnik's shadow. The mass hissed and pulled back. It fell down on the grass and turned back into a cat.

My cousin's face twisted as he looked at the dagger. "What the f—"

I materialized next to him and struck out with Sila, aiming for the back of his neck.

The blow never landed. With a puff of smoke, Golo was gone. I wrenched Veter out of the panel and whirled, daggers in each hand. The ovinnik hissed at me. Its howl pierced the air.

In response to it, other black shadows stepped out from behind the trees. They slunk out of bushes and jumped off roofs. More and more gathered on the grass. Their eyes filled with fire and flame rolled out of their mouths. Everywhere they walked, the park grass smoldered and smoked.

There were too many to count and their hissing filled my ears.

"Good kitties," I said as I backed toward the building. "Let's all take a deep breath."

Where was Golo?

The ovinniks pounced. Their fist-sized claws extended toward me, and this time I didn't have Coria and Tynan to watch my back. I struck out with Sila and Veter, but these weren't sirins or even the drekavacs. Quick and agile, they moved too fast to make good targets. In seconds, two of them sank their teeth into my jacket. Their freakishly big kitty claws beat and scraped against the sleek fabric. I saw the fire that rolled between them stop as their fire retardant did its thing. That gave me a second to bash one against the brick wall to my right. The cat fell and snarled. The other one spat out my sleeve and slid down my leg to my jeans. I yelped in pain, then kicked it away.

More came at me and I swore at my lack of foresight. I was what the gamers call a "glass cannon." Someone who dealt a lot of damage from far away, but shattered like a Chinese vase at the hit of a hammer. I wasn't a melee character, damn it. Which meant that I had to be harder to catch.

My right pant leg caught on fire. I looked down and yelped as two more cats fought for the right to tear off my balls as they went after the much more burnable denim. Not wasting another second, I tossed Veter at a sycamore tree and shot past the mewling hell kitties.

Their eyes couldn't follow me and their ember irises blinked stupidly at the spot where they'd last seen me. Perched on a low-hanging branch, I slapped out the fire on my calf. Grinning at their confusion, I decided it was time for payback.

I tossed Veter at the nearest ovinnik. As always, it hit true. The dagger went exactly where I aimed it—right in the center of the fire monster. Except that it didn't.

Morphing from solid to the black glue I'd seen earlier, the ovinnik melted away from my dagger. It materialized two feet away, unharmed, and spitting. Frowning, I tried again. And again. All of my throws came to the same result. I did nothing more than piss them off. What was more, I gave away my location. As they prowled toward the sycamore I was perched on, I realized that I was a moron. Who hides in a tree from a bunch of fire cats?

Desperate, I looked over the buildings for anything that I could drive Veter into. The campus buildings were pitilessly absent of anything remotely good for holding a dagger. The cats were at the foot of the tree and where they climbed it to get to me, orange flame crawled over the bark.

Not having a choice, I chose another sycamore that was further away. Air whoomphed out my chest as I caught myself on a branch. I searched the ground for Golo, but didn't see a sign of my cousin. Where could he possibly be?

It took the cats only a few minutes to locate me again. Their superior eyesight pierced the dark and snapped to the smallest of movements. I had minutes, if not seconds until they were on me again. My daggers were doing jack shit to them. I needed another solution. A non-magical solution.

As the first sycamore went up in flames, something red caught the corner of my eye. I zeroed in on a fire hydrant. An obvious, if far-fetched idea split my mind. Water and fire cats? If normal cats hated the spritz, the ovinniks were probably even more vulnerable. I remembered hearing somewhere that their natural habitat in Vyraj was always away from rivers and lakes. It was worth a shot. The tip of my tongue between my teeth, I sent Veter flying.

The hydrant sparked as the dagger ricocheted off the metal. I swore as dozens flaming eyes followed the sound. Then, as quickly as before, they zeroed in on me. Veter wasn't strong enough to pierce it. Luckily, I had the perfect tool for the job in my left hand.

The fire hydrant sat in the corner of the courtyard. Walls rose around it. If someone—say, me—was stupid enough to get trapped there, there would be little way out. On the other hand, I wouldn't be the only one with my back to the wall.

Instead of calling Veter back, I climbed down the tree as quickly as I could. The ovinniks were far enough away that my mad plan could just work. Or maybe I was running toward my death. Only one way to find out. My jacket billowing, I sprinted to the fire hydrant.

Meowing, hissing, and snarling followed me into the corner where the two buildings met. Stooping, I picked up Veter as I ran. I halted next to the fire hydrant.

"Here, kitty kitties!" I yelled into the night. "Come and get me!"

No sooner than the words were out of my mouth, feline shapes in dark fur spilled toward me. I backed as far as I could manage as ovinniks pressed me to the wall. I waited until enough gathered. Then, striking out as if my life depended on it—which it did—I sliced the outlet cap with Sila. The power dagger cut through three inches of metal like it was paper.

The water exploded. I flung myself away a split second before the pressure could wrench my arm out of my socket. White, billowing gush shot out with the force a semi-truck. Through the fog and the noise, I saw it sweep ovinniks off their feet and shoot them across the lawn. The aggressive hissing was replaced with yowls. Fire turned to vapor as the water smothered the fire cats' magic.

Drenched, I crawled away from the hydrant. I climbed to my feet and whirled around, checking for threats. The ovinniks were too busy being shaking themselves out and disappearing into the night to care about me. I would have whooped in victory, but that's what kids did. Instead, I pumped my fist like an adult.

The water was shooting thirty feet across the lawn. It spilled over the roots of the sycamore trees and began putting out the one ovinniks were burning down. I hoped the tree would make it. Salt Lake was short on historical artifacts as it was.

Pulling off my jacket, I wrung it out. The water sluiced off the shimmery fabric. Beneath it, my shirt was only a little wet. I backed away from the water, sheathed the needles, and began shaking out the jacket.

A smoldering hand grabbed my throat from behind. I choked and struggled. My skin sizzled and the stench of my own burning flesh filled my nostrils.

"Very clever, cousin," Golo snarled into my ear. "Too bad you weren't clever enough to stay home."

I felt smoke crawl up my body as the two of us burst into flame. My fingers loosened around the fire retardant cloth. Grabbing me across the chest, Golo dragged us somewhere else.

22

WHEN WE MATERIALIZED ON the other side of the building, I gasped for air and came up short. The flames licking our bodies went out, leaving smoke. Golo was in front of me, teeth bared. Blistering hand on my throat, he slammed me into the wall. Above us, a campus building smoldered. Flames began spilling out the windows and crawling onto the roof.

We were about the same height, but he was wiry where I was well-muscled. By the laws of physics, there wasn't supposed to be any way his tweaker frame could support hoisting me into the air. But there we were, a fully-fledged demigod that was over a hundred years old, and me. Little ole me, dangling like a puppy from his grasp. My fireproof jacket was left in the water. Not that I thought it would do a damn thing now.

He sighed as he watched me struggle for breath.

"Please tell me you decided to come across town just to save me a trip," he said. "I have things to do."

"Like... burning... the city?" I rasped.

He grinned. Smoke rose off his jacket. "Caught on, did you?"

Lifting me off the wall, he threw me on the grass. I sprawled out.

"I guess I really have to kill you now," he said. "Babushka will be disappointed."

I rolled onto my back. The skin on my throat was blistered. "As... if... you were going to let me... live."

Golo shrugged his shoulders and lit a cigarette. "I thought about it. You chose the wrong day to suddenly get brave. I'm already not in the mood." His head tilted up as he took a long pull of his cancer stick. Smoke rolled between his teeth. "I'll just have to collect the needles from your cremains." Thrusting up his hands he made two fists and smashed them together. Old magic burned my nostrils. "Say "hi" to auntie Dolya for me."

A wave of heat made the hair at the back of my head sizzle. Golo's manic giggle turned into a full-blown witch's cackle. His tongue flicked between his teeth as he stared behind my shoulder.

I turned in the direction of his grin. The building had turned into an inferno. A snake head rose out of the flames. It opened its maw and its teeth flared down like two blow torches. Its head was the size of a fridge, and its serpentine body was searing the school announcement sign to ash. A heap of embers stirred and another head, a twin to the first one, lifted out of the fire. The two-headed snake screeched, fire spilling it out of its maws. A fire zmei narrowed its eyes at me.

Oh. Mama.

One giant snake head lunged at me like a falling tree and I struck the ground. Rolling, I swore as the wound on my bicep opened. Burning grass hit my nose and I was blinded by the smoke. I scrambled to my feet and started past the floating embers onto the street. I heard Golo's laugh behind me. Screw him, I thought.

Leaves crunching under my feet, I started down the lawn to the safety of the non-flammable asphalt. The ground exploded as the twin snake head snapped the air in front of my face. Heat blasted against my eyelids and cheeks, and for a horrible instant, I was blinded. I stabbed the space in front of me but struck nothing.

"Wooo!" Golo shouted. "Get 'em, cousin! Work that cardio!"

I struck out again and was deafened by a scream. Falling back, I was grateful Min-Ho made me spar with him three days a week. My body moved on reflex, twisting out of the way and landing in a crouch. Being further away, I could finally see. The snake coughed up flames and I saw a gash on its jaw. I didn't celebrate landing my target. By the looks of it, I only managed to piss it off. While it was distracted, I quickly searched the grounds for its sibling. I spotted the second snake slithering toward me. Its glistening orange body left a fire trail through a bed of petunias. Ignoring the angry screams of the snake behind me, I aimed, and let Veter fly.

Dolya's needle whistled through the air and into the snake's eye. It hit like a bullet. The dagger lodged deep inside the socket. I'm no expert on reptiles, but I'm pretty sure that's where the brain is. The fire snake bucked and its long body coiled. Blinded, it snapped its teeth at the area of my proximity, spitting balls of fire. The ground under my feet flared up. My sneakers smoldered and I stomped down the flames that reached up to engulf my jeans. The snake's body retracted into itself as it howled. It slacked like a rope and folded into a coil. Then, with a sound like shattering glass, it burst into shreds of ember.

"Eb tvoyu mat'!" Golo swore in Russian from across the lawn. "You asshole!"

The snake's skull dissolved into coals and I felt a burst of heat as its brother spat flames at my back. I smelled my shirt burning, and beneath it, my skin sizzled. Pain split my skull and the ground shifted beneath my feet. I stumbled, then ran across the lawn to what remained of the snake. Pulling my sleeves over my hands, I raked through the coals.

"Better hurry, cousin!" Golo's voice was triumphant. I kept searching, not wanting to give him the satisfaction of looking up. In the steaming remains of the snake, my dagger, now a needle, smoldered red-hot. I hesitated. Reaching deep into the embers would hurt like a mother, but the hissing behind me told me I didn't have time to kick away the pieces. Doubling my sleeve over my palm, I thrust my hand into the embers.

Lightning-hot teeth sank into what remained of my shirt and my feet left the ground. I felt the serpent's fangs burn into my spine as the lawn beneath me grew smaller. Golo's face beamed at me from the sidewalk. The snake lifted me over the trees. I kicked and wiggled. Its teeth sunk deeper until I couldn't feel my back.

Golo's hands cupped his mouth. "See you later!" he yelled.

I stabbed blindly behind my back with Sila. The burning roof caught my sneakers on fire. I felt wind in my hair as the serpent swung me deeper into the inferno. Looking through the fallen roof, I saw a classroom that was still intact — an oasis of unburned desks and, blessedly, a window. I looked down at my unfeeling right hand that I'd thrust into the embers. The needle had burned through the remainder of my shirt and had seared into my blackened palm. As the classroom inched out of reach, I willed the needle to turn into a weapon. Veter swelled in my palm as the ancient metal changed shape. I bared my teeth in pain and grasped the bloody handle. Spinning the left dagger into position, I thrust both blades over my head.

I felt the daggers pierce soft flesh and strike the skull beneath. The snake's skull was too hard to break through, but its startled cry seared my hair. I felt its teeth loosen their grip and twisted. Something popped and suddenly, I was in the air. I wish I could say that I landed like an anime hero, feet hitting the ground with a cloud of dust, fists clenched and wind in my hair. Instead, I crashed onto a desk like a sack of wet bones.

"Owwwee."

I hurt all over. The plastic seat barely missed my crotch. Small mercies. I pressed my cheek against the blessedly cool wood of the desk. Whoever said that fire was cleansing had never spent time in the mouth of a fire serpent. I couldn't imagine the state of my back, and decided that it was best to focus on living long enough to complain about it to a nurse. I made myself stop clutching the seat like it was the door in Titanic and slid to the floor. Flames crept down the walls and the roof creaked above my head. The window that I had glimpsed on my snake roller-coaster ride was to my right and I began to army crawl toward it, daggers in my fists. The roof sighed over my head and I moved faster, crabbing as furiously as I could, as every instinct I had told me that certain death loomed, literally, over me. The window was just within my sight, blessedly open and waiting for me. Burning shingles showered my head. I kept crawling, legs kicking.

The only thing that separated me from the world of the living was a short stretch of linoleum. I kicked my legs and did my best ignore the agony in my right hand and back. I could smell fresh air cutting through the smoke as the roof caved in.

I crashed and rolled through the window. When I landed, shattered glass covering me like a sugared donut, Golo stood over me.

He blew smoke in my face and clicked his tongue.

"Oh, Dmitry," he said. "No wonder your last name's Kozlov. Stubborn as a goat." He leaned over me for a closer look. "A sacrificial one."

Pain threatened to blind me, and his hollow-cheeked face blurred in my vision.

"Why don't you," his boot landed on my throat, "just die already."

The daggers in my hands were useless, and the pain intensified as my cousin took his sweet time squeezing the life out of me. He was right. What had I been thinking coming there? I wasn't sure what I had expected to happen. Did I think that I could somehow outsmart the demigod that had been operating in full power for decades? He probably felt no hesitation in claiming his god-powered status in Vyraj. I was glad I didn't let Coria and Tynan come with me. At least this time, my pride would only cost one life. Mine.

Something shimmered in the distance. I thought the lack of oxygen was making me loopy. Then, I realized that at edge of the lawn, another one of my stalker portals had opened. The damn thing rippled with inter-pantheon magic, beckoning and swaying in my blurry eyesight. What the hell did it want? Gamayun's voice sounded in my head.

A bond that stretches out through the fabric of the world. It is reaching for its missing piece.

Missing piece. My god-power lay unclaimed. And it was powerful enough to tear through realities.

How had I missed this before? It seemed so obvious now. I *was* the reason the portals were opening. They were opening because my demi status lay unclaimed. It was missing a piece of itself. That piece... it was me.

With a guttural howl, I drove Sila into Golo's left foot.

My cousin yowled and fell back. Throwing my shredded, aching body with all my might, I grabbed his ankles. This time my superior weight made a difference. With a crashing thump, I drove him down to the ground.

Golo kicked at me. "What are you—"

I grabbed him around the knees with my left hand. My right hand cocked Veter. I released the handle and let the wind dagger zoom into the portal.

For a second, Golo and I stared at each other. Then, I grinned a bloodied grin. Veter disappeared between the sizzling edges. Sila connected with its twin. We were shot through the fabric of reality.

23

WE FELL ON THE lush grass of a birch grove. The pink sky above us was a deep purple, hinting at a sunset. The portal sizzled and closed with an electric snap. No sewing up necessary. It must have gotten what it wanted.

Golo's combat boot smashed into my chin and I rolled off him. He scrambled to his feet. My hot forehead met cool grass. The sensation in my body was as if someone had worn me like a puppet and then thrown me into the gutter. I clutched my daggers to my stomach. In seconds, they reverted back to needles. I couldn't feel them in the burned palms of my hands.

"What the hell did you pull?" Golo sniffed. He dragged the heel of his palm across his bruised cheek where his face had hit the ground. "What difference does it make?" He shook out his shoulders like a wet dog. "I'll just kill you here."

If Vyraj had wanted my blood, I thought, it had plenty now. My multiple wounds seeped into the ground. My mother's needles were just two sticks of metal between my fingers. I couldn't feel the power in them.

"My ovinniks will finish the job," he said. "You think they only burn shit when I tell them to?" He snorted and patted his pockets. "You made me lose my smokes!"

I barely heard him through my ringing ears. My fingers released my needles and clutched the dirt beneath me. It felt soft as velvet. Welcoming. How had I missed how good it felt before? Now that I was here, I realized that I made this choice last night in the kitchen, back when I wasn't sure if Alysa would live or die. The moment I chose to find Golo before he found me, I already knew. Too bad my lungs were burning from the smoke and my throat felt like raw hamburger. Otherwise, I would've enjoyed a long, ironic laugh.

"Hey." Golo's footsteps drew him closer. "What are you doing?"

My cracked lips opened just wide enough for a whisper. I pressed my bloody palm to the grass.

"Blood to earth, earth to blood," I rasped in Old Slav. "Let my bond make me god."

"Answer me!" he roared and kicked me in the ribs. "You stinking piece of—"

A ripple shook the ground and Golo jumped back. His face went from annoyance to amazement to fear.

"What did you—" He paled and the dark circles under his eyes made him look like a corpse. "You wouldn't!.. You can't!.."

My body *expanded*. It seemed to soak up the earth beneath me and the sky above me. I felt like a vessel being filled and stretched to bursting. My needles no longer felt separate from my palms. They felt like a limb. I felt my wounds shrink and close with a satisfying ache. My skin sizzled with energy. The headache in the back of my neck shrank to a dull thud.

"You wouldn't dare," Golo hissed, as if trying to deny reality that pointed to the contrary. "You're too much of a coward."

My spine cracked and I choked on a moan as my body jerked straight. I wanted to laugh like a maniac. Lying on the ground, I felt amazing. Was real-life instant regeneration a thing? I felt like it was. Full bars, baby.

I pulled my knees under me, no longer feeling like tenderized pork loin. My elbows on the ground, I panted, trying to work through the sensation. I didn't know how I felt, and I didn't know what I was. Luckily, *who* I was hadn't seemed to change. I was the same idiot that had followed his overpowered cousin to his death. Except, I wasn't a puppet anymore. Now, I was a real boy.

My daggers slid across the grass without me having to reach for them. All it took was a mere thought. Veter felt slimmer and longer. Sila was heavier and its blade was jagged now. I wanted to take my time and feel them. Feel *myself*. But I had more pressing things to do.

I rose. My hair fell into my eyes, and I glowered at Golo through my soot-stained bangs.

"It doesn't matter!" Golo spat on the ground. "I can still take you."

He dodged Sila as it sang over his head. My dagger felt him fall away and it followed him down. The hilt crashed into his windpipe.

Golo staggered and clutched his neck. He threw out his palm and a fire ball swelled over his fingers. His stained teeth bared at me.

"Come and play, big boy," he hissed.

I didn't bother informing him that he sounded like a gay porn flick.

Veter sang past his ear and pierced the birch tree behind him. He looked back at it and grinned.

"You missed, asshole."

Oh, but I didn't.

The string that connected the daggers was no longer a string. It was a wire rope. Holding Sila, I wrapped it around my wrist and pulled.

The birch came crashing down. Golo looked up just in time to skitter out of the way, but a few branches lacerated his jacket. I stared dumbly at the earth-clustered roots.

"Holy moly," I breathed. With a jerk of my hand, Veter dislodged and flew to me. I caught it, marveling at the long, needle-point blade.

I was pulled out of my reverie by a fireball hitting my shoulder. I staggered back, the pain blinding. Golo looked at me expectantly, as if he was waiting for me to go up in flames. Instead, the ache dulled and I turned my shoulder in its socket to test it. Other than burning the sleeve off my t-shirt, the fireball didn't do much damage.

"Nice shot," I said to him. Golo paled.

I could throw things, too. With a twirling spin from behind the back that surprised even me, I let Veter fly at Golo. The way it pierced the air should've been impossible. It was so fast, even I could barely follow it. Veter pierced Golo's shoulder with a satisfying slurp. My cousin bellowed, and pulled it out. He didn't toss it away fast enough. I followed it with Sila.

The weight of my body slammed into him. I bore him into a birch that stood on the inner edge of the grove. He howled in pain. Veter slipped from his grasp and fell on the ground. His palm looked blackened from it. That was new.

My right hand clutched the front of his raspberry jacket. I lifted him off the ground. In my left, Sila pressed against his Adam's apple. His right hand circled my bicep and I felt his fire crawl over my skin.

I gave his head a little thump. "Stop it," I said calmly. "We're a little past that, don't you think? Unless you want me to test my strength."

His hand dropped to his side.

"You wouldn't kill me, would you cuz?" Golo's smile was bloody. "That wouldn't be sporting."

"Depends on whether you piss your pants," I said and wrinkled my nose.

He laughed. "You don't know what you've done. Now, we're all screwed." He ran his tongue over his teeth. "It's too late to fix it."

"Fix what?" I asked.

He didn't answer but his smile broadened. I smelled cigarettes on his breath. "Either kill me or let me go."

I hesitated. A part of me—the part that was still sobbing tied to that tree, watching my childhood home burn—wanted to drive my dagger through his neck. A tiny whisper of sanity told me my junkie cousin wasn't worth it.

"Call off the ovinniks," I told him. "Now."

He closed his eyes and I saw his eyeballs move under the lids. "Done."

I released him and he slid to the ground.

"Get out of here," I said. I was exhausted. Even with the new power humming in my blood, I still felt like taking a long bath and a nap. "And I better find my city intact."

"Your city?" He pressed him hand to his shoulder wound and stared up at me. "Aren't you back in Vyraj now?"

"My city," I repeated. "My home. You come for my home again, and I'll come for you."

I turned around and began to walk. I half expected a fireball to be hurled at my back, but Golo settled for threats.

"There are a lot more of us than you," he called after me. "Only your mother could keep me and my siblings at bay. And she's dead now. How can *you* handle us?

I turned back to him. Since I didn't have an answer to that very excellent question, I flipped him off.

Golo cackled and threw out his arms. "Till next time cousin. And I won't come alone."

Flames enveloped him and his body dissolved in their midst. In seconds, he was gone.

As the woods closed around me, I realized that I had no way to get home. I sat on a tree stump and stretched out my legs. The daggers were still intact and I turned them back into needles for easier transport. Really, I could just go to grandmother's and wait for rescue. There was no reason to delay a visit now. But I didn't feel ready. I had to at least shower and bring some flowers—and a bottle of my best wine or two—to apologize to the matron of Vyraj.

A strange surge hummed through me that had nothing to do with the fact that I felt like a—albeit bedraggled—Superman. Despite Golo's very legitimate threats, and the fact that I had just made the most dangerous choice of my life, I felt whole. Stitched together. I felt like I finally made sense.

I tucked the needles away and wiped my hair from my face. That's when I noticed something that definitely wasn't there before. A golden glow came from my right hand. In the encroaching dark, it was obvious where it was coming from. The lifelines of my palm were glowing. I frowned, and thought it looked familiar but couldn't remember where I had seen it before.

A loud tearing sound came over my head and I looked up. My body reacted with just a second's delay, ready to face the next threat. Instead of an army of drekavacs with all of my cousins at its head, I stared at the unnervingly calm face of Agent Killian. He stepped out of a rippling portal and gave me a cryptic smile.

"Dmitry Kozlov," he said in a three-tone. That's right, he was some weird hive mind straight out of Black Mirror. I had all but forgotten about the Spiral. "I have finally found you." Two identical copies of him stepped left and right of the primary body. They wagged their index fingers at me in a three-fold reprimand. "It's not smart to run from the universal law."

"Oh, good," I said. "The cops are here." I crossed my fists and thrust them out toward him. "You got me! Drag me away to Vyraj, officer!"

He and his clones clasped their arms behind their bodies. Idly, as if seeing his surroundings for the first time, he glanced around.

"Ah," he said. "I see. Sarcasm."

"Can you always find me like this?" I asked. "Even in other pantheons?"

"Sometimes," Killian said easily. "We felt the portal leak close, and it drew us here. And here you are, as I suspected you might be."

That was unsettling. I needed to investigate the exact extent of their GPS tracking using the drop of my blood. And maybe steal it back when I had the chance.

"They won't open anymore," I said.

Killian inclined his head. "Then, Ms. Lapina has nothing to fear from us."

I rubbed my aching forehead. "I'm going to assume I'm still not welcome in Yav."

"On the contrary, Mr. Kozlov," Killian said. "I'm here to welcome you back. Agent Frónima would like a word upon your return."

"I bet he would," I said.

"In the meantime." Killian stepped aside and extended his arm to the portal, like a steward waiting for a passenger to board the plane. "Would you like a ride home?"

24

Dust sparkled in the beam of light that fell through the open door. My lungs inhaled the musty, woody scent of the warehouse. My face split by a manic grin, I stepped over the threshold. The key was warm in my palm. I hadn't stopped holding it since the realtor had said "sign here," and that was four days ago.

"The American Dream," I said to myself. "Congratulations, Mr. Kozlov. You're a business owner."

The empty shelves lined the walls and looked like they needed to be replaced. The floor needed a good sweep and the high windows had more spiderwebs than glass. I didn't care. I wanted to move in a cot and spend every waking moment cleaning, repairing, and building.

There was one new thing that shone with its round chrome finish. The industrial fermenter sat under the window where the delivery crew had placed it. It was the shape of a tear-drop, eight feet tall, and had a valve that made it look like a vault. I'd spent the last three days in Las Vegas at a brewing trade show. Savings burning my pocket, I'd splurged on this beauty. After James picked me up from the airport, I had to go see it immediately. My first real piece of equipment. I wanted to throw my arms around it and weep.

"Cool," James said behind me. Ever the poet, that one. My friend held the door open to let in fresh air. His eyes glittered as he surveyed the space. "You can throw such a rager here."

I grinned. "Don't even think about it."

"Come on, man," he said. "A little house warming party? It's good luck."

"Yeah, we'll see."

I walked the length of the shelves. This is what I'd wanted for years. I was just as elated, more even, than I would've been a week ago. But something had changed. *I* had changed. Instead of something that I needed to hide, this investment became something I needed to protect. Something that, along with my home and new-found family, I had to fight for. It felt more precious than ever.

Checking the kitchen area, I made a mental note to replace the sink with a double. It needed a rinse-off area, too, and a drain. There was so much to take care of.

Running my hand through my fresh haircut, I took a deep breath. Don't lose it, Dmitry. This would take a lot of work, and a lot of money. I had a long way to go. Still, the road burned my feet and I couldn't wait to get started. I really didn't want to lock up, but my suitcase of dirty laundry and three days of eating bad buffet food needed to be addressed.

James drove us home in his daddy-bought BMW that was too nice for a twenty-five year old. When we turned down our street, he suddenly looked uncomfortable.

"Oh, yeah," he said guiltily. "I forgot to tell you something." He shifted in his seat. "We have... Well, you'll see."

I narrowed my eyes at him. "I'll see what?"

"It's a surprise," he said sheepishly.

We pulled up next to the house and my eyebrows rose at the pile of suitcases that sat on the porch. They looked straight out of a music video—black leather, horns, metal buttons and spikes.

Metal music poured from the open front door. I recognized James' voice in the speakers. Whoever was inside was playing Overkyll. I threw a dirty look at my roommate and grabbed my suitcase from the trunk. He bared his teeth in an awkward smile. What had he done without informing me?

Before I got up the steps, the door swung wider. Coria stood in the frame. Her hair in a topknot, she wore black yoga shorts and a sports bra. She held a box in her hands.

"James," she said. "Your band is not very ba-" She blinked when she saw me. "Oh, hi, Dmitry. Welcome home."

My roommate coughed behind me. "Surpriiise," he said.

"Hi, Coria," I said. "What are you doing here?"

"Oh." Her eyes went between me and James. "I'm moving into the spare bedroom. James said it was okay."

I looked away from the stunning dark elf that looked like a model from a treadmill commercial and back at my oldest friend.

"I'm sure he did," I said. James had the decency to color.

She pushed past me. "Excuse me," she said, "I have to rinse these out."

Something glass clinked together in her box. My guess was they were beakers.

As soon as she was out of earshot, I whirled on James.

"What the hell, man?" I demanded. "You discuss these things with me."

"Look, look," he said quickly. His hand grabbed my shoulder and he pulled me into a circle of conspiratorial whispering. "She's gonna be great for our brand, right? I mean, she's metal as hell. And have you seen her—" He briefly closed his eyes. "Wow."

"I've seen her, James," I said, my face stony.

"We're gonna be the hottest house in the city," he said. "We can get people from all over to come and party. Tony Skin, Black Moss--" He began counting off his favorite indie bands on his fingers. "Sky's the limit, man."

I wondered what my air-headed roommate would say if he saw his new crush tear into a sirin in her werewolf form.

"Hey, by the way." James glanced over his shoulder to make sure Coria was still far. "Is that Tynan guy her boyfriend or what?" he asked.

My lips stretching into a smile, I didn't tell him that Coria was gay. All I wanted was to be there when he found out on his own. Hopefully, it would be soon. And in public.

I slapped him on the shoulder, and gave him an encouraging smile. "Why don't you find out for yourself, buddy? I'll put in a good word for you."

He nodded enthusiastically and thumped me back with a pervy grin. "Sweet, thanks dude!"

Still smiling, I watched him disappear into the house. Sweet, sweet revenge. I just hoped he came out of his investigation with his balls intact.

Coria came up the stairs. She held a sponge in her hand and her arms were wet to the elbow. I quirked an eyebrow at her.

"Why the heck—" I started then shook my head. "Just why?"

She leaned against a pillar. "Thanks to you, I have more monsters in my inventory than I've had in years," she said. "And now that you've claimed your powers, more of your cousins will come. They will bring their creatures."

"Thanks for the reminder," I murmured.

"Aid for you." She pointed the dripping sponge at my chest, then stuck a thumb toward herself. "Monsters for me."

"And your armiger?" I asked. "What does he think?"

Her face darkened and her red eyes darted sideways. "He's not my mothers. He doesn't get a say."

I nodded. "That's what I thought. Can I expect to wake up with a slit throat?"

"No," she shook her head. "Of course not." Her brows knitted and she cocked her head, considering. "I don't think so, anyway."

Great. I sighed and lifted my suitcase over the threshold. "Rent is due on the fifth of every month," I said.

She brightened. "Noted, demigod."

I dragged my suitcase downstairs. As much as I loved the latest development in my life, I didn't have much time to dwell on it. Once in the basement, I threw my clothes in the washer. I smiled when I thought about Domo freaking out that I didn't separate the lights and darks.

I took the time to tidy my room and took a long, sudsy shower. Clean and cologned, I found a nice button-up shirt. I checked my reflection in the mirror. Not too bad for a guy that looked like road kill just a week ago. Going through my cupboards, I slid a bottle of concord red wine into my backpack. After a thought, I added a peach white, and a strawberry rosé. There was no such thing as too much booze for the amount of butt-kissing I had to do tonight.

When I was finished with my preparations, there was a pop in the hallway outside my room. A knock followed. Crossing over the carpet, I opened the door for Alysa.

The shifter wore a pair of khakis and a loose, flowery blouse. Her blue hair was shiny, curled, and fell to her shoulders. I cocked an eyebrow at her.

"Are you going to an interview?" I asked.

She made a face. "Like you're not nervous."

Touché.

I slung the backpack over my shoulder. "Ready?"

She nodded. With dizzying speed, she transformed into a ferret. I stretched my arm out and she hopped on. The room blurred and in seconds, we weren't in my basement anymore.

The sun had already set in Vyraj, and the velvety blue of the night was warm and fragrant. The pines and birches were black silhouettes against the sky that never quite got as dark as in Yav. This time, we were closer to our destination than Alysa usually portalled us. I could tell by the twinkling blue lights that lit the path to Baba Yaga's house.

Shifting my backpack to a more comfortable position, I walked toward the chimney smoke that pillared in the distance. This time of night, Baba Yaga's hut on chicken legs would already be settled for the night, and the old matron of the forest would be in her kitchen, fussing over a stew.

Tomorrow, my cousins could bring an army of monsters to take me down. The Spiral could decide that I was more of a threat than a benefit to the city and kick me out. Hell, Coria could take offense at James' advances and turn my best friend into a lobster. Tomorrow would be tomorrow. I shifted my shoulders under the comforting weight of the ferret. Her tail tickled my cheek. Tonight, I was going to visit my babushka.

THE END

Continue on to read the first chapter of BOUND: Kozlov Chronicles Book 2

KOZLOV CHRONICLES

BOUND

ELENA SOBOL

NEXT TIME WHEN YOU feel like a real bad-ass, check yourself. It's entirely possible you're about to fall on the aforementioned ass. Bad.

I sure felt pretty cool when I drew my mother's famous Bow of Fate. Veter, the wind dagger, was my arrow. Sila, the strength, had turned into the golden body of the bow. Shimmering with its multi-hued fibers, the string that tied my daggers together glistened in the sunlight. I breathed through my nose and out my mouth like Leshi taught me. The god of the forest had been drilling archery into my head for the last three months. My eyes focused past the string and on the target.

"You can do it to-to-to!" the wood spirits chanted in broken unison. Their twiggy wings buzzed as they struggled to keep the block of wood in the air. It took three of the little fae to hold it. The others whirled around like overgrown dragonflies. Was that as dangerous as firing a cannon at a bowl of fruit? Yep. But hey, they insisted, and I'm not a Supernatural Creatures Endangerment Committee. "Fire, Master Dmitry, fire to-to-to!"

You gotta give the people what they want.

Exhaling, I let Veter fly. The arrow only vaguely resembled the dagger I was used to, but it sang through the air with familiar surety. At first, anyway. Then, it did something it'd been doing for weeks. The opposite of what I wanted.

The arrows split fifteen different ways. Instead of one exact shot, the dagger turned into projectiles that wobbled as they turned to aim at everything in sight.

The Sila bow bucked in my hands. It hit me on the mouth hard enough to wobble my front teeth and send me flying back. From the ground, I saw the arrows hit every tree, boulder, and bush in the clearing. The shrill of escaping wood sprites filled my ears. Explosions deafened me. My hands wrapped around my head. I curled up on the ground, praying to Veles to allow me to be the exception to the rule and *not* shit my pants as I got blown to bits.

When the bangs stopped, I opened an eye. All I saw was smoke. A gentle breeze tugged at my hair and my clothes. Feeling like I'd just been crushed by a tractor, I stumbled to my feet.

A patch of green grass surrounded me. Sila lay at my side. The blade smoldered. I picked it up, hissing as the hot handle burned my palm. Switching it back and forth between my hands like a hot potato, I slid it into its sheath.

The birch grove was flattened. Stumps of trees smoked against the blue-and-pink sky of Vyraj, the Slavic pantheon. I looked around for the heart-wrenching sight of small sprite bodies, but there were none. Thank the gods for that. The patch of green around me looked suspiciously uniform. What had protected me? I wiped the blood off my upper lip and only then noticed that I wasn't alone.

A woman watched me with attentive blue eyes so pale she looked almost blind. White hair cascaded down her shoulders and her nose ended in a distinctive hook. She looked anywhere between sixty and a thousand years old, yet no one would be dumb enough to call her "old." The woman looked as immune to time as a pyramid. She leaned on a staff that vaguely resembled an over-sized pestle. Baba Yaga, the supposed eater of children, destroyer of princes, and an absolute terror of the Slavic world smiled at me. Her expression of pity was mixed with tenderness. It made me feel like even more of an idiot.

"In one piece, are you?" she asked. "I just received my grandson back. And there he goes blowing himself up."

"Thanks, Babushka," I said. After three months of regular visits, my Old Slav was smoother than it had been in years. Small mercies. "Sorry I flattened another grove."

The walk back to my grandmother's house was a bit of blur. The chicken hut was resting in the mid-summer heat. When I was six years old, I'd named the hut "Kura," which literally meant "chicken". I wasn't a very imaginative kid. Its legs half-buried into the warm soil below, the magic hut barely moved as we approached. When I came back home in June, it had remembered me. And a good thing, too. Once, I saw it kick a trespassing troll a hundred feet in the air. We never saw the troll again.

"Hut, hut," my grandmother said. "Turn your back to the forest and your front to me."

The ancient spell rippled the air, and the hut lowered its porch in front of us.

"You should rest, Dmitry," Baba Yaga said. "I'll make us tea."

Bless that woman.

My vision stopped spinning somewhere between the front door and my room. I barely found my way to my wooden four-poster bed. Around me, my old room was as Spartan as it had been when I was growing up—a single window that shone light on the wall carpets, the slanting ceiling, a simple chest for clothes, and my mother's portrait. I collapsed on top of the covers and let dizziness take me.

When I came to, I saw a wood sprite hovering over me with a bloody towel he'd just lifted off my face. The charred state of his wings made guilt nibble my guts. I took the towel from him. After almost blowing him up, I could dab my own damn lip.

"Are your friends ok?"

He chirped and did an awkward mid-air flip. "We are quick to-to-to!"

I sighed. They were quick the last time, too. And the time before that. Ever since my cousin Golo almost burned my human city to the ground, I'd been training night and day. Back in June, I'd claimed my godpower after almost a decade of dodging my demigod responsibilities. The result was that I had a target on my back. My cousins, the children of Likho the One-Eyed, the goddess of bad fortune, were coming. Today, tomorrow, or months from now. I was the only thing standing between them and the world. Unfortunately, claiming my legacy had made my trusty daggers go wonky on me. I sat up on the bed, and took my mother's ancient needles from their sheath. With an effort of will, I turned them into a pair of daggers.

Sila, the power dagger, now carried a jagged edge. Veter, the wind dagger, was slim, sky-blue, and practically weightless. I'd used them for years. Now, they felt foreign in my hands.

When I came back to Vyraj, my grandmother explained that my mother's primary weapon was something called a Bow of Fate. One blow from it turned wrong into right, and slaughtered enemies in droves. I believed the "slaughtered" part. I was also pretty sure that blowing up acres of the forest wasn't supposed to happen. At least I was much harder to kill these days.

Until I mastered my mother's weapon, I was as good as useless. More than useless. I was a gods-damned health hazard.

Looking up, I found my mother's portrait over my bed. It was the same as I'd remembered—a beautiful stranger with a braid over her shoulder and the classic Slavic features of a tall forehead and wide-set eyes. Now that I was grown, I recognized the shadow of worry in her expression and the determination in the line of her angular jaw. I had inherited both. Dolya had a lot resting on her shoulders. When I was a kid, I saw tenderness in her face. Today, I only saw her failed expectations. I swung my legs out of bed.

"Today was a disaster," I said to no one in particular. "I really need to stop messing up."

"Perhaps, Master Dmitry, something isn't quite right to-to-to." The sprite buzzed around the room like a giant mosquito. I had almost forgotten about him. "You should play to your strengths maybe to-to-to?"

"Yeah, and what's that?" I asked. "Flattening vegetation?"

The smell of frying potato made me drift toward the kitchen. A towel to my lip, I pushed open the door.

"Smells good," I said.

Baba Yaga looked up from the stove and her chin bobbed. "Your favorite, Dimmy."

I sat at the long wooden table and looked beyond her hunched form into the rest of the house. It was as deceptive as my babushka's ordinary appearance. There was nothing ordinary about the Yaga's hut. For starters, it was about four times bigger than it looked from the outside. Etchings covered the walls. They were spells that were older than time. Even the herbs that hung over the wide-mouthed stove were deceptive in their cozy appearance. Half of them could kill a herd of elephants. At night, the hut turned into a neon cave lit by mushrooms ravers could only dream of. And yet, that wasn't the weirdest thing about the hut. Sitting on top of the can-lined shelf was an honest-to-gods microwave. I had no idea where my grandmother had gotten it or why. It's not like the pantheon full of gods and monsters ran its own electric grid.

"I saw you walking around again last night," Baba Yaga said as she placed a steaming plate of potato hotcakes in front of me.

I smeared a layer of sour cream over the steaming disks. My stomach nudged me at the smell. Mmmm.

"I just needed some fresh air," I lied.

Her spatula struck my clavicle.

"Owe," I murmured.

"Don't lie to your babushka," she said.

That almost made me smile. I rubbed my shoulder and admitted:

"Had that nightmare again."

"The one with the wolves?" she asked. I nodded. "You know your cousins can't hunt you here. My wards won't allow it. You have to sleep."

"Once I get the Bow of Fate down, I'll sleep," I said.

"You're wearing yourself thin." She piled three more hotcakes onto my plate, then poured mushroom sauce over the small mountain. "Eat more."

I grinned. My friend Min-Ho, a Korean goblin and the meanest gym partner on the planet, would have a conniption if he knew how many carbs I ate in Vyraj. Then, I remembered that it was Sunday night, and I'd have to go home soon. I stuffed my face with a vengeance.

She watched me eat with the tenderness only grandmothers are capable of. I had to admit that I had missed her care. Had starved for it in the eight years I'd dodged my responsibilities. Three months ago, she had taken me back without hesitation. Unfortunately, my cousins knew where I lived now. But then on the flip side, I got babushka's cooking back.

"Your mother lives within you, Dmitry," she said. "You will find her power, even if it takes years."

I shrugged and swallowed another oily, potato-y, delicious bite. Somehow, it didn't taste as blissful as ten seconds ago.

"Somehow," I said, "I doubt I have that long."

A knock came from the door, and my grandmother snapped her fingers. It opened by itself, and the doorway revealed a girl with blue hair that fell to her shoulders. She froze with her fist in mid-air.

I smiled at her puzzlement. "Hey, Alysa,"

I looked at my phone. Here in Vyraj, it mostly served as a brick, but it still ran the time in Salt Lake City, my human home. It was already eight pm. I had to open the warehouse tomorrow, and fill an order heading to a brewery in Moab. All by my lonesome, because thanks to my shitty karma lately, nobody wanted to work for me. And I thought Golo was the demigod of bad luck.

I gathered my backpack, hugged my grandmother, and headed outside.

"Come back when you can, you hear?" My grandmother waved from the doorstep. "And by Veles, lad, get some sleep!"

Alysa and I walked the glade that separated the hut on chicken legs from the Mavki Forest. The blue-pink sky had turned the violet of dusk. Now that I was a full demigod, I could teleport to Vyraj straight from my bedroom in Salt

Lake City. My house spirit, Domo, and I made enough energy to step between realities without Alysa's help. Unfortunately, it didn't work in the other direction. First time I tried to go home from Vyraj on my own, I had ended up in a no-name village in Slovakia. The locals were very confused. Apparently, I could only travel back to Yav in places where the belief in the old Slavic gods was strong. After a brief stint at the local police station, I was able to call Utah. Thank the gods for international cell phone plans. Alysa came and got me, then laughed all the way home. That was the benefit of being the only living portal on earth. The world was her oyster.

"How's training going?" she asked with a pointed look at my split lip.

"Oh, you know, peachy," I said. "Flattening groves, blowing out my knees. Running out of time. I need a beer, like, yesterday."

She snorted. "Luckily, you have an entire warehouse of it. Have you found someone to take your nights, or are you still pulling double shifts?"

I rubbed the bridge of my nose. "Can you please stop asking me about my failures? Kinda rude."

"What about that guy last week—Wayne something?" she pressed. "I thought he was wetting his shorts to do part time."

"He mysteriously disappeared," I said sourly. "Well, not that mysteriously. After two interviews and dropping off his cactus, he texted that he was offered another opportunity."

"Did you keep the cactus?" she asked.

"You know I did," I said. "As compensation for emotional distress."

She laughed and I looked at her from the corner of my eye. Ever since our scrape with death in June, we'd been more at ease with each other. She'd started hanging out at my house just because. That had never happened before. Sometimes, when she turned into her animal form—an adorable blue ferret—she napped in my garden. I couldn't pretend I didn't like it. We were still friends, but it was different somehow.

My fatigue was suddenly gone. "Should we go for a walk?" I asked. "I kinda dread going home."

Her face changed as her eyes shifted to me. Uh-oh. She thought I was flirting with her. Was I?

"I thought you were in a hurry," she said.

"Well, I just thought—"

My attempts at covering up were rudely interrupted by a burst of flames on our path. Smoke billowed up in the air. A dark shape materialized and I'd be liar if I said I didn't squeak.

A giant fire cat, and one of Golo's thralls, stood in our way. I recovered quickly, daggers at the ready. Alysa ducked behind my shoulder.

Fire rolled out of its eyes and lit the tip of its tail. Its maw opened over a sharp row of teeth. I was expecting one of its horrible guttural meows, and got an even nastier surprise. A voice, that sounded smokier than a can of sardines, came slithering out of its mouth.

"Time's up cousin," Golo's coughing chuckle filled my ears. "One is coming for you. But who? *Who are you, who, who, who, who?*" he sang in a creaky baritone.

The transmission from its master delivered, the ovinnik rushed me. I shielded myself and Alysa with crossed daggers. I already knew from experience that throwing things at the pyro cat was pointless. Two seconds before a blistering collision, it exploded into a shower of sparks and flared up into the sky. I watched it disappear.

"Now," I said to Alysa, "I *am* in a hurry."

AUTHOR'S NOTE

Thank you for reading STITCHED! For an independent author, reviews are extremely important, since they lead to better visibility. Besides, I want to hear from you! If you liked the book, please consider leaving a review on Amazon or Goodreads.

To keep up with Dmitry's shenanigans and learn more about the nerd behind the man (me) sign up for my newsletter on my website www.elenasobol.net

See you next time!